AFT'ER the WAR

Russian
Zone

Buchenwald

U.S. Zone

Fr.
Zone

French Zone

Innsbruck
ALPS
Merano

POLAND

Lodz
Kurov
Ostrowiec
Kielce

Katowice

Klodzko
Nachod

CZECHOSLOVAKIA

Bratislava

U.S.
Zone
Vienna
Russian
Zone
AUSTRIA

Saalfelden
British Zone

HUNGARY

YUGOSLAVIA

ITALY

ALBANIA

GREE

U.S.S.R.

ROMAN

N

SCALE

100   0   100   200 miles
100   0   100   200   300 kms.

Designed + produced by P. Heersink/Paperglyphs

AFTER THE WAR

CAROL MATAS

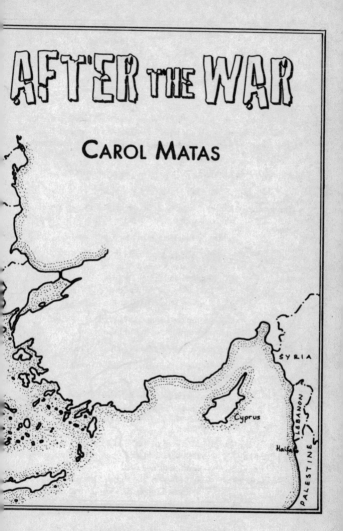

Aladdin Paperbacks

First Aladdin Paperbacks edition September 1997

"The Immigrant Experience" (on page 9) copyright © 1994 by Per Brask, reprinted with permission of the author.

Map by Paul Heersink/Paperglyphs

Aladdin Paperbacks
An imprint of Simon & Schuster
Children's Publishing Division
1230 Avenue of the Americas
New York, NY 10020

Also available in a Simon & Schuster Books for Young Readers edition.

Printed and bound in the United States of America
10 9 8

The Library of Congress has cataloged the hardcover edition as follows:
Matas, Carol, 1949–
After the war / by Carol Matas.—1st ed.
p. cm.
Summary: After being released from Buchenwald at the end of World War II, fifteen-year-old Ruth risks her life to lead a group of children across Europe to Palestine.
1. Holocaust, Jewish (1939–1945)—Juvenile Fiction. [1.Holocaust, Jewish (1939–1945)—Fiction. 2. Jews—Europe, Eastern—Fiction.] I. Title.
PZ7.M423964Af 1996 [Fic]—dc20 95-43613 CIP AC
ISBN 0-689-80350-8

ISBN 0-689-80722-8 (Aladdin pbk.)

To Donna Babcock and Tim Babcock with heartfelt thanks, and to their children, Jennifer, Jordan, Jeremy, and Hilary

Acknowledgments

I have many people to thank, particularly those who gave me their time and shared their stories with me: Pinchus Levine, Tzvi Farens, Joe Lerer, Simon Slivka, Aryeh and Bernice Mellor, Shmuel Segev, Nachemia Wurman, Henry Melnick, and Israel Eichenwald who sent me his memoirs from Israel and who actually told the Gorky story I use in my book to his Brichah people, in order to inspire them. Also and especially to Pnina Zilberman, Director of Holocaust Education and Memorial Centre of Toronto, and Dr. David Bleeman, who were of invaluable help in locating survivors of the war.

Many thanks to Perry Nodelman for his perceptive critique of the manuscript, and to David Gale, my editor, who was always a delight to work with; to Nina Thompson at the Winnipeg Jewish Public Library, who was always generous with her time; to my mother, Ruth, who helped me find people to interview; to Margaret Krzysanska for her excellent work as my researcher; to Bill Connelly at the U.S. Holocaust Memorial Museum Library, who supplied me with a bibliography; to my husband Per, who listened, as always, to the book chapter by chapter as it unfolded and never stopped encouraging me; to Tim and Donna Babcock, Donna, who typed the manuscript, Tim, who helped ferry it back and forth and was always there to help solve computer glitches; thanks to my editor at Scholastic Canada, Diane Kerner, for all her support. Finally, to the Manitoba Arts Council for the award of a Major Arts Grant which made the travel and extensive research possible.

THE IMMIGRANT EXPERIENCE

*like warriors of fate they delivered themselves from
hell leaving fires behind they sought water*

*braving mountains in winter and hostile neighbours
they were illegal everywhere*

*carrying their small inside coats taken from the dead
they knew even deserts would learn to grow trees*

*trusting no one they could see the path ahead
no longer the scorched of the earth*

—PER BRASK

Chapter 1

"I thought you were all dead. Didn't the gas ovens finish you all off?"

By "you" I know she means "you Jews."

And then I realize who it is, standing in the doorway to my Uncle Moishe's house, glaring at me as if I am some kind of disease-carrying rat. It is Brigette. She used to work for Uncle Moishe as his maid. Now, I suppose, she lives in his house as if it were her own. And the dress she is wearing—where have I seen it? Involuntarily I gasp as I realize it used to be Mother's. Black with white lace around the collar, Mother wore it for Shabbat dinners, always with a string of gleaming white pearls, her black hair braided on top of her head, pearl earrings dangling from her ears.

Father would come to the Sabbath dinner in his black suit, the table would be covered in white lace, the silver candlesticks would gleam as Mother lit the candles, illuminating the china, the fresh flowers, and our faces all scrubbed and clean waiting impatiently for a taste of Mother's famous fish, chicken soup, and roasted chicken.

Why do I have to remember such things?

"That's my mother's dress," I blurt out.

She starts to shut the door. I leap up the steps and

put my foot in, so she can't.

"Have you seen anyone?" I ask. "Uncle Moishe, Fagey, Benjamin, Joseph, Rachel?"

She shakes her head.

"Anyone from *my* family? My father, my mother, Joshua, Simon, Hannah?"

She shakes her head at each name.

"This isn't your house," I say fiercely.

She shoves me back from the door and spits. "It is now! You were always a troublemaker, Ruth Mendenberg. Always."

The door slams in my face. I feel weak and so I sit down on the cold step, shivering. Now what?

City hall. If anyone did survive they would register with the local authorities. I force myself up and begin to walk away from my uncle's house. I take one last look.

I was born there, it was the family home in Ostroviec, but Father moved us to the small town of Kurov when I was only three years old, so he could start his own business, a store. Everyone worked and helped in the store—even me, but only when Mother could lay her hands on me. Mostly I'd hide in the woods reading my favorite books. I did just enough schoolwork so no one could fault me for poor grades, but any time not spent with my Zionist youth group was spent daydreaming, making up fantastic stories of dybbuks and ghosts. At night I scared even my older sister Hannah as I whispered tales of graveyards and the walking dead to her and my older brothers, Joshua and Simon.

Dybbuks were souls of the dead, wandering, searching for a human body to inhabit—sometimes I pretended to be possessed, other times I would pretend to see the dybbuks entering my sister or my brothers. The boys laughed and pretended not to be scared but I could tell that sometimes Simon couldn't sleep after one of my stories.

Father moved us to Uncle Moishe's house after the entire Jewish section of Kurov was destroyed by Nazi bombs in September 1939. But we were there for only a short time. Soon we were forced into a ghetto, a small run-down section of Ostroviec with all the other Jews of the area. That's when the roundups began.

When we lived in the ghetto Hannah often begged me to tell them stories at night. But I couldn't think of anything scarier than real life anymore. Especially after the day most of the Jews were herded into the town square and shot. Father hid us under the floorboards of the house we were staying in. Others had escaped somehow, too. Those of us who lived were put to work in factories. Until we too were taken away.

Smoke endlessly seared the sky overhead. Mother and Hannah were marched off. Perhaps it was their ashes that fell on me later in the day, as the ovens and crematoria of Auschwitz blazed and burned.

I hate these memories, they jump at me just as a ghost in a graveyard would leap out at you from behind a gravestone, when you least expect it.

I have to ask a number of people the way; many

won't answer me, but I finally reach the city hall and I am directed to an older man sitting at a desk covered with paper.

He smiles at me. "The government is trying to help," he says, after I tell him why I am there. "Name?"

"Ruth Mendenberg."

"Mendenberg. Mendenberg. Let's see." He goes through his files, searching for the name, searching to see if any other Mendenberg has registered. I try to keep my stomach quiet, try not to let the butterflies start, try not to get my hopes up. Finally he looks at me, shakes his head.

"What about your mother's side of the family?" he suggests.

"Lepidus," I answer. He checks again. Shakes his head. My legs are beginning to feel wobbly. I can barely stand. He notices and finds me a chair. I sink down into it.

"Your father's mother's side?"

"Saperstein."

Again he checks.

We try every family name I can think of. Nothing. Nothing. Nothing.

I feel I'm going to suffocate. The noise of the office sounds like a roar to me, every sharp noise like gunfire. I need air. I mutter a thank you, get up, race out of the building, and sink down on the cold steps of the city hall. I am shaking. I should have asked him about a place to stay. I should have asked him for help. I'll have to go back in there. But I can't face his look of sympathy; I don't want to see him again as he shakes his head and tells me over and over that I'm all alone. I put my head in my hands. What am I to do? I have no education, I can't work. I have no one to live with. It's dangerous just to wander around. Do I return to the displaced persons camp I just left?

"*Amcha*," a voice says. I look up. A tall young man stands in front of me. He has black curly hair, high cheekbones, big dark brown eyes, and his skin is olive colored. He looks healthy and strong—not like the usual survivors of the war.

I know what *amcha* means. "With the people," literally. It's Hebrew and is used as a code word. If someone says it to you, he can be trusted, because he's one of us, one of the people, a Jew.

"*Amcha*," I reply. He holds his hand out to mine. Slowly I place my thin cold fingers into his strong warm grasp. He pulls me to my feet.

"Have you just arrived in Ostroviec?" he speaks in Hebrew.

I nod.

"I thought so. I check here regularly for people like you. Come with me. We've set up a house for refugees. You look done in."

I know I should let go of his hand. But I grasp it like it is a lifeline. And he doesn't seem to mind.

"Where are you coming from?" he asks as we walk.

"First a hospital near Buchenwald," I reply. "I was sick for a long time. Then I was in a D.P. camp for a while. I tried to find my relatives through the Jewish Agency but I couldn't. Or they said they were dead. But I kept hoping. . . . I had to come back to Poland and see for myself."

He nods, as if he's heard this story before.

"I went to my hometown of Kurov first," I continue. "But, of course, there's nothing left there. Our house was bombed in the first days of the war—that whole section of town is still rubble. And then I came here. My father brought us here in 1939 to live with my Uncle Moishe. I was hoping maybe someone from my family would return here, too." I pause. "My uncle's maid is living in his house now. She's wearing my mother's dress. If I had the strength I'd rip it off her with my bare hands."

"You don't seem all that weak to me," grins my companion, as he glances at my iron grip on his hand.

I think I blush and I release his hand from mine.

"Your Hebrew is very good," he comments.

"I was in a Zionist youth group from the age of five," I reply. "My older sister, Hannah, was the president. We were allowed to speak only Hebrew. That was her law. And my parents sent me to Hebrew school every afternoon. I wanted to learn Hebrew. I wasn't interested in much else. I wanted to go to Eretz Israel, to Palestine."

"I'm from Eretz Israel," my friend says, casually, as if it was an everyday thing.

I stop in my tracks, and stare at him. I'm actually walking with someone from that land, the land I dreamed of, the land we spoke of in the concentration camps as some sort of paradise.

"I'm a Sabra," he says. "Born there, lived there all my life."

"What are you doing here?" I ask.

"I've come to help people like you immigrate," he replies. "We check with the Jewish Agency to see who registers, we find people any way we can, or they find us." He looks at me. "We need you in Palestine—to help us build a Jewish homeland."

"You need *us*?" I can barely contain myself. "No one needs us. No one wants us. We're just dirt that's left over from the war to be swept away whenever possible. Dirt."

He looks me in the eye.

"I don't want to hear you talk like that again. You've survived. You've beaten the Nazis. You've ruined their plans to kill all the Jews. And now we need you in Palestine."

I know he is wrong. I haven't beaten Hitler. He's beaten me. Before the war there'd been almost eighty in my family, aunts, uncles, cousins, grandparents. Now? Am I the only one left? And if so, why me? I don't deserve it. Or maybe it is my punishment for being the bad child of the family. Doomed to live when everyone else has left me.

Why did I survive?

Chapter 2

We arrive at a house on the main street. As my companion leads me into the house, it's obvious to both of us that something is very wrong. He hurries into a large sitting room, just off the hallway, which is full of people. I lag behind, trying to make sense of the scene.

A young woman, in her middle twenties I'd say, is screaming and tearing at her hair. Another woman of the same age sits beside her on a couch and weeps, silent tears coursing down her face which is completely devoid of expression. Three or four young men, also in their twenties, are in various states of distress as well. One cries, another mutters angrily to himself, two others talk earnestly to each other, having some kind of discussion or disagreement. An older man, perhaps in his midthirties, and a woman of the same age are trying to calm the others down and trying to get information from them. When I look closer I can see that one of the young men has a bloody nose, another a nasty cut on the head, the women's dresses are torn, and they all look rather bruised and battered.

My companion, although obviously younger than most of them, commands respect the minute he strides into the room.

"What has happened?" he demands, looking to the older man and woman for answers.

The man replies, "A pogrom, a pogrom."

My new friend looks grim. We all know what pogrom means—the slaughter of Jews.

"Any dead?"

"Five," the woman replies.

"Who?"

"Karl, Borov, Krista, Yakov, Lenni."

My friend walks over to the hysterical young woman and grasps her hands so she can't hurt herself. "Make some strong tea," he instructs. "We must think what to do."

The older woman hurries past me to get the tea. Within minutes everyone has quieted down and silence falls over the room. Then the older man notices me.

"Who is this?"

"Ruth," I answer, walking into the room.

"I found her outside the government buildings," the young man says. "The maid lives in her old house now," he adds.

I sit down on a wooden chair, one of many in the room. The young man who has been muttering to himself looks up and notices me.

"Come to join us?" he says, his voice bitter. "I wouldn't recommend it."

"All the more reason to join," my friend says, over-hearing the remark. "It simply makes it more obvious that your only choice is Palestine. A Jewish homeland where no one will ever hurt you because you're a Jew." He speaks fiercely and with conviction.

"You're right, Saul," one of the other young men says. "But how do we get there before we're all killed!"

Another pipes up. "We've spent enough time here in our little kibbutz, pretending it's a real kibbutz in Eretz Israel. We train, we prepare—no more. It's time to go."

The older woman comes in with tea and everyone gulps some down. It's very black and very sweet. The young man beside me begins to talk.

"We were having a Hebrew class, in our house a few blocks away," he says, "when out of nowhere the doors burst open and about twenty thugs burst in. They beat whoever they could and dragged those five out in the courtyard and shot them, screaming 'filthy Jews, Commie tyrants,' that sort of thing. I'm pretty sure they're part of a fascist group that's been terrorizing the local government. The police came, but too late, and made some arrests. That's it."

The older man speaks. "It's too dangerous here now. They may come back. Maybe even to this house. Perhaps the rest of your group should go to Kielce. There are about 200 Jews there now, many of them organized into kibbutzim. And Saul can contact you there when we're ready to go." He suddenly seems to remember me. "Ruth, you don't know who any of us are. My name is Shlomo, and this is Leena," he says, pointing to the older woman. "This is Kirstin," he says, gesturing at the girl who'd been hysterical; "this is Miriam," he continues, pointing at the quiet one; "this is Nate," he points at the fellow who'd been crying; "and here we have Pinchus, Zev, and Jan." He looks at me.

"How old are you, Ruth?"

How old are you?" the lean-faced S.S. man looked at me, the wrong answer meaning death, the right one maybe one more day of life. One more day, or week, or month, as a slave.

"Fifteen, sir," I lied.

"Very small for fifteen," he scoffed. "But strong." He sent me to the left. To work.

"How old are you, Ruth?" They are all staring at me.

I consider. They are all young men and women in their twenties. I know I'll be the baby but I don't want to be too much the baby.

"Seventeen."

I can be whatever age I want. I have no papers. All the teenagers who've survived are so small and stunted in their growth that most seventeen-year-olds look no older than twelve. I've grown a bit since I left the hospital but no one can tell from looking at anyone what their age is. I don't want to be treated like a kid just turned fifteen. So I lie. I'm used to lying. Lying has helped me survive.

"Maybe you should go with them," Shlomo says. "It's obviously not safe here right now."

I shrug. I don't care. I'll go with them to Kielce if that's what they want. But travel to Palestine? What for? A better life? There is no such thing. That was just an empty childhood dream. Life is nothing, is meaningless. Here is just another example. These people had somehow made it through the war, had come here, perhaps like me looking for family, had found no one, then had found one another. They'd joined a kibbutz, a communal organization, they'd trained for a life in Palestine, and then they'd gotten murdered! Life is worthless, I've learned that. But I don't have anywhere else to go so I agree with their plan. Why not?

"Good, fine," Shlomo says, when I nod my agreement. "Go pack your things," he says to the others. "We'll put you on the train this evening."

I have my rucksack with me. All it contains is a mug, one change of clothes courtesy of the Jewish Agency, a comb, and a brush. Within an hour we are boarding the train to Kielce. Saul holds my hand for a moment as I step into the train.

"Come to Palestine," he says. "You *can* start over."

I don't answer. I know he means well, but who can start over when memories never leave you? The train begins to move.

The train began to move. There were over 100 of us in the cattle car. People screamed and cried. I held onto Mama and Hannah. Simon begged me to tell him a story. Simon was only a year older than I. We were very close. I gave in. I made up a story of a friendly ghost who hid in the ground, rising up to play pranks on the unsuspecting bigwigs of the town. Soon it played pranks on the Nazis. Their guns began to fire backward. And their orders came out all scrambled so that they were marched into camps and only had one another to shout at, to beat, to kill, and finally they destroyed each other and . . .

"Ruth. Ruth. We're here."

I'd fallen asleep. Nate is drying my face with his sleeve. "You've been crying," he says softly.

I nod. I cry only in my sleep. Since the war began, not once have I cried while awake. I was ten years old when we moved into the ghetto. One of the first things I learned was that there was no point in tears. Tears didn't help you survive.

Someone meets us at the train station in Kielce and we are quickly taken to Planta Strasse, No. 7, the Jewish Community's house, where we are to stay until the next morning when we'll find other accommodations. We're given tea, bread, and some cheese and then all of us fall onto the mattresses which have been put down in one of the upstairs rooms. My fellow travelers are exhausted from the terrible ordeal they've been through. I'm exhausted because it looks now as if all hope is finally gone. How is it possible? No one left but me? Could they *all* be dead? I think of Simon, with his black hair and blue eyes—people often thought we were twins—and how he used to scold me for not working hard enough but he never, never, gave me away to Mama, Papa, or my teachers. Mama, Joshua, and Hannah had all been listed as dead at Auschwitz. Father, dead on the death march. But of Simon, there was no record after Auschwitz. I had hoped.

That was stupid of me, of course. I will never hope for anything again.

Chapter 3

We are all sitting in the common room. It's a lively house, full of cheerful people, activity, resolution. A committee of Jews works from here, trying to help people like me search for their families. There is also a kibbutz of young people in the house. There is a steady flow of people from the house to Lodz or elsewhere, and then presumably on to Palestine. The operation is called *Brichah*, which is Hebrew for "flight" or "rescue," and I learn that Saul is a Brichah organizer sent from Palestine to help anyone who wants to immigrate there. The more Jews they have living there, the stronger is their case for a Jewish state.

Nate and Miriam talk about how the British have betrayed us. Before the war and during the war when the Labour Party was in opposition they'd promised to open Palestine to legal immigration. But as soon as they were elected they broke their promise, more worried about Arab oil and the Arab aristocracy than the remnants of European Jewry.

Nate tries to convince me to join their kibbutz. It is called Noar Zioni, and in fact is the same one that I belonged to as a child. Politically it is middle of the road, neither left nor right; its leader, David Ben Gurion.

Miriam jumps up and runs to the window. "What is that noise?" she asks.

It is faint at first but gets louder and louder. It sounds like thunder or rain on a tin roof. Everyone hurries to the window. People have begun to pour into the street in front of the house. Hundreds of people, with more coming all the time.

"Oh, dear God," murmurs Miriam. "It's happening again."

Kirstin begins to scream. "They'll kill us. They'll kill us all."

"Stop it!" I say to her. "Come on. We must hide." I look around, frantically. "Don't you have a hiding place? A secret room? Floorboards?"

The occupants of the house shake their heads. I'm disgusted. Don't they know they *always* have to have somewhere to hide? Jan motions everyone to be quiet as he looks out onto the street, and listens to the angry shouts and screams.

"It's bad," he says, turning to us. "The police chief is *with* the mob. So are some soldiers. They're armed. Listen."

We listen at the window, which is open a crack. I see a little boy—he couldn't be more than nine years old—screaming, "That's where they kept me. The Jews kidnapped me and they held me in their basement and they murdered my friends and they are using my friends' blood for strange and horrible things. This is the place. They held me there all night.

They made me watch when they slit the children's throats."

The mob becomes more and more inflamed. Suddenly a rock crashes through the window, then the crowd surges forward. I look around frantically, and see that the couch offers a little protection. I throw myself behind it as I hear the door break with a terrible crack and people pour into the house. Kristin screams horribly and I hear Zev and Nate and Jan yelling as they fight with nothing but their bare hands. The room is turned over and trashed but no one bothers with the couch. For a moment there seems to be a lull, but I can't tell what's happening and then I can hear more people crashing up the stairs. The upstairs doors have been barricaded, I can tell from sounds of the crowd trying to break them down, and then there are gunshots and screams as people are dragged down the stairs. Finally the house is quiet, but the noise from the street is horrible.

I creep from behind the couch and move to the window. The crowd is beating some of the occupants of the house, using bricks, sticks, or stabbing them over and over with knives, all the time screaming, "murdering Jews, filthy Communists, child killers."

It looks like there are thousands of people in the street, all after this tiny helpless little group. A few manage to escape back to the house. Zev is one, Nate another, Miriam another. I look around. The couch. I begin to push it toward the door. Would it fit through the inner door quickly enough though? Just then the three manage to get in and slam the door behind them.

"Quick. The couch," I shout. We push it up against the door.

"That'll hold them for a bit," Nate says, his voice shaking. "The director called the military for help," he adds. He pauses. "Before the mob broke into the room and shot him."

The crowd once again begins to pound on the door so we all run up the stairs. It's a terrible scene up here. There are dead and wounded everywhere.

"Get some sheets for bandages," Miriam orders. "They'll all bleed to death if we can't help them." Pinchus lies in a pool of his own blood, obviously dead. I'm not sure who the others are. We rip up sheets and try to help whoever we can. The banging on the door is getting worse.

Suddenly we hear shouts, and shots are fired outside and the pounding stops. I run to look out a window.

"It's soldiers. The government has sent in soldiers," I say.

As I look down into the street I can see Kirstin and Jan lying on the cobblestones. A soldier checks them, one at a time. Then he shakes his head. Both dead.

Finally the mob disperses and the soldiers come in. We move the wounded to the mattresses on the floor that aren't ripped or blood soaked. I do what I can to tend to them. A dozen or so Jews stagger into he house. Their house has also been attacked and they report that a crowd had found some Jews at the train station and attacked them, too.

There is nowhere that is safe. But somehow I've survived again. I don't know how to stop.

When the doctors and nurses take over, I fall asleep on the downstairs couch. Nate wakes me to tell me that the wounded are to be taken to Lodz to be treated. He asks me if I'll go along with him and Miriam to help out. Why not? I have nowhere else to be.

When we arrive in Lodz and the wounded are settled in the hospital, I am taken to a house to rest for the night.

Saul is waiting for me in the kitchen, sipping tea.

"Hello, Ruth," he says.

I nod to him.

"I have a job for you."

I sit down at the table and accept a cup of tea offered by one of the young people staying there.

"I have a group of twenty orphans we need to get over the border into Czechoslovakia and from there to Austria. We have good camps set up in and around Vienna. The children can't stay here anymore. You wouldn't go alone. Miriam has volunteered. So has Nate. What do you say? Will you go?"

I shake my head. I can't help anyone. Not even myself.

"Come with me," Saul says.

I follow him into a room filled with little bodies fast asleep. They range from the ages of six to perhaps fourteen or fifteen. Many toss and turn, cry out in their sleep. I wonder how the little ones have managed to survive with no parents.

"Some of them were in convents or orphanages disguised as Christians," Saul says. "Some hid with their families or older brothers or sisters in the forests. They need our help."

We go back to the kitchen.

"Do you have anything better to do, Ruth?" he asks.

I look at him. He knows I don't.

"You'll be too busy to—remember—," he says very softly.

That's as good a reason as any. He is clever, Saul. He knows people's soft spots.

"All right," I say. "I'll go."

"You'll leave first thing in the morning," says Saul. "Better get some rest."

Chapter 4

I sleep fitfully, my cries intermingling with those of the youngsters in the room next door. We are woken while it is still dark, and fed a breakfast of bread, jam, and tea. Saul gives Miriam, Nate, and myself instructions.

"We'll put you on a train to Katowice. There you'll change for a train to Klodzko. From there a truck will take you to Kudowa. You may have to sneak the children across the border at night into Czechoslovakia. Once there we have papers for you, all looking very real, naming your entire group as Greek refugees returning home. Speak only Hebrew—the border guards don't know the difference between it and Greek. And *don't* let any child who *can't* speak Hebrew speak at all. That'll give you away.

"You'll be met on the Czech side and taken to Nachod to be processed. From there to Bratislava. Then on to Vienna and finally, if we can manage it, we'll get you to Italy and then on board a ship to Palestine!"

I try not to show it, but I am impressed. And I know that this will be just one of many routes the Mossad Aliyah Beth will be using. All over one hears of secret routes to Palestine.

"The most dangerous part," Saul warns, "will be crossing the border on the Polish side. We're going to give you cartons of cigarettes to use as bribes, but sometimes it's better just to try to sneak across. The guards could take the bribe and still not let you over."

"Or shoot you," Miriam says quietly.

"It's been known to happen," Saul acknowledges.

"If you fail, you can always come back here and we'll try again—maybe we can get you papers to go across 'legally,'" Saul says. "These kids have been in Lodz for five months. We've taught them Hebrew, sung songs with them, given them classes in agricultural training for life on a kibbutz in Palestine. But we can only do so much for them. They are determined to go to Palestine. It has given them something to live for. And now we have to help them make their dreams come true."

He looks at me then as if he knows how I scoff at the word "dreams," as if he wishes he were talking about me.

The children are ready to go, waiting for us in the main room downstairs. The older ones each have a younger one in tow, their eyes gleam with excitement.

Saul introduces Miriam, Nate, and me to them, and goes with us to the train station. He waves as the train pulls out of the station and smiles, and I realize that my heart is beating quickly: Perhaps the adventure we are about to begin is making me feel different. I try to squash the feeling as quickly as possible.

I am in a compartment with ten of the kids; Miriam and Nate are in another compartment. The children look at me, expecting something—I'm not sure what.

A little girl sitting beside me gazes up at me and asks me my name. "Mine is Leah," she says, "which means 'to weep,' but I never cry. Do you?" she asks.

"Never," I reply.

This seems to satisfy her and she now feels that I am a fit companion.

"Where are you from?" she asks.

For a moment I am confused. Does she mean where was I born? I hadn't been in my hometown for six years. Is that where I'm from?

"Nowhere," I reply.

"Me, too," she answers, seeming happier with that answer than my first one.

I begin to find her quite interesting.

"Where did you spend the last few years?" I ask. "Before the war ended," I add.

"In the forest," she replies, in a matter-of-fact sort of way.

"With your family?"

"Family?" She rolls the word around in her mouth then grimaces. "They were killed in an 'Action' when the ghetto was cleared out. I ran into the forest."

"How long were you in the forest?" I ask, astonished despite myself, because she's so young.

"A long time," she answers solemnly. "I ate mushrooms and roots or I stole potatoes from the fields at night. Once a group of fighters found me and let me stay with them. They took care of me. They were Poles. Then the bombing started and I got separated from them and finally some Jews from the town came out into the forest and found me. They found most of us," she said, gesturing at the group.

"Were you all in the forest?" I ask.

Some shake their heads, no.

"Where then?"

One boy hid in a small space in a barn for years, with the help of Polish neighbors. Another ran from town to town, barn to barn, place to place, always just ahead of the Nazis.

A young girl sitting across from me says, "They used to sic the dogs on the town whenever they thought some Jews might be hiding. But I used to run into the river and stand there so the dogs couldn't smell me. One night the dogs caught two of my friends and ripped them to pieces."

Just then Miriam comes into the compartment.

"What's this?" she says. "You all look so serious. We're on our way to Eretz Israel! What about a song?" And soon she has the children singing and clapping.

The trip to Klodzko is uneventful. We get the children off at the station and are met by a Brichah driver who hurries us onto a truck, headed for Kudowa. It is a beautiful summer day. The sky is blue, the hills and forests are deep green splashed with flowers. There is some beauty in the world, I think to myself, if only in nature, certainly not in people. Although I *am* impressed by how smoothly these Brichah workers have everything going so far. We reach Kudowa near dusk. The Mossad operator who drives the truck points the way to us, across the border, assuring us someone will be there to meet us if we make it through. We line the children up in twos, always an older child escorting a younger one. There are a couple of girls my age, I think, a couple of boys too, but I don't let on for a minute that I should be *in* the group, not leading it.

It is dusk when we lead the children through a path in the forest to an open meadow. There, past the high grass, over to the right, we can see the frontier: two posts about 100 yards from each other, each manned by soldiers.

"I don't think we should risk going anywhere near the posts," I say. "We don't know how the soldiers will react."

"We do have cigarettes to bribe them with," Nate reminds me. "Why don't we try?"

I don't like the idea. My hunches had often helped keep me alive and I had learned to listen to them.

"No," I say. "Let's wait until it's dark and then cross there, by those houses. *Away* from the guards." I point to a cluster of three or four houses where the ground is cleared and where we can hurry across in the dark. The grass is too high and thick for the children to cross beyond that, and dense forest stretches on the other side.

Nate and Miriam look at each other. They are older than I and in charge.

"I'm going to try to bribe them," Nate decides. "If it doesn't work, you two take them across."

I can see there is no point in arguing with him. He is gentle and quiet but obviously tough in his own way. I remind myself that he'd have to be to have survived.

He walks down the road in full view of the guards. I see him talking to them. They appear agitated. He brings out some cigarettes. One of the guards seems to relax, takes the cigarettes. The other grows even angrier. He makes Nate sit down on a chair and then I can see him using his telephone.

"That's it," I whisper to Miriam. "They're going to arrest him."

They pull his hands behind his back and tie them to the chair.

"It's up to us now," I mutter. "I *told* him not to go!"

"Now what?" says Miriam.

She is tall and really quite beautiful, if nervous all the time. She wrings her hands and picks at her skin, and tugs at her hair constantly.

"We have no choice but to go through the village," I say. "We'll wait until dark when everyone down there is asleep and then make a run for it."

She nods in agreement, then settles the children on the forest floor. We have all eaten on the train, bread with salt and a little margarine, but I am hungry and thirsty by now as I'm sure all the children are. Still, none of them complain. And they are absolutely quiet, even the littlest ones of five or six.

When the moon is well up in the sky and we are all shivering we decide to move. We walk through the grass over some small hills until we reach the top of the rise just before the hamlet. We begin to descend when soldiers, laughing, cursing, and swilling liquor, pour out of a house below us. I motion everyone to the ground, and we flatten ourselves in the grass. The soldiers clamber onto a cart, continue to talk and laugh, and begin to shoot their guns. From this close I think I recognize the two from the border post.

I realize that we are stuck. We can't go back—they might see us. We certainly can't go forward. All we can do is wait until the soldiers decide to leave.

But I have another idea. I crawl over to Miriam.

"I think those are the two from the border post," I say. "I'm going to go over there and try to free Nate. You stay here with the children. If I'm not back when these idiots leave, just go across without me."

Miriam has half the papers that Saul had given us but Nate has the rest. We need the papers, I tell myself. But the truth is I can't stand the thought of any Jew being tied up, made a prisoner. Not now.

They were rounding up Jews in the ghetto. Pulling them out of the houses, shooting them on the spot. I heard my cousins scream as they were taken away.

They hadn't managed to hide in time. When we crawled out of hiding, little Rachel was tied to a chair with a rope. Her own socks stuffed in her mouth by some guard had suffocated her.

I crawl through the grass which is quickly becoming wet with dew. It takes me a long time to get to the border post. Once there, I raise myself to my knees and peek around. Nate sits tied to the chair, but no one is watching him. I get up and run over to him. He grins when he sees me.

"There are some bottles in the hut," he says. "They've been drinking."

I nod, run in, find an empty bottle, break it on the ground, and begin to cut through his ropes, which are very thick. It takes me at least fifteen minutes of arduous careful slicing until I finally break through. Once free he grabs my hand and shakes it, then forgets that and kisses me on the cheek.

We scramble back through the grass to where I'd left the others. Nothing has changed. The soldiers are still drinking, firing their guns into the air, and generally having a wonderful time. The dew is thick on the ground by now and the children are shaking with cold. We worry about stray bullets hitting someone but there is nothing we can do but wait.

Finally, the soldiers hitch their carts to their horses and begin to drive off. The two guards from the post begin to stagger back toward it. We all know that once they notice Nate is no longer there we'll have no time at all. The second they are far enough away we motion to the children to get up. The moon is setting and the light is now very poor but we have no choice. We forge ahead as quickly as possible through the high grass into the little town. A dog begins to bark crazily.

"Who's there?" calls a voice.

We grab the little ones and run.

Furious shouts come from the border post. A shot rings out behind us as the sun breaks over the horizon. And we can see we are across the frontier parallel to the Czech border post! But then Czech guards are running over to us, rifles pointed.

Chapter 5

I can see a truck parked just beyond the Czech border post. A short stocky man gets out and watches intently as Miriam and Nate show our documents to the Czech guards. Nate speaks to the guards quickly, in Hebrew. This is more or less what Nate says:

"You are stupid idiots and probably couldn't tell if we were from the moon but we're not from the moon although many of us feel we're from another planet, after what we've all been through, but we're not *Greek* we're Jews but you don't know the difference and that's great or you wouldn't let us pass now and we are really tired and cold and wet and hungry."

He says all this with a big smile on his face. I look at Nate closely for the first time. He is short, very skinny, with thick brown hair which waves off his face, brown eyes, a narrow nose, and a wide thin mouth. He isn't good looking exactly but he looks sharp, like he knows what he's doing. I notice the way Miriam is looking at him, sure he'll get us across, and I suddenly realize that she likes him. But she's so much taller than he, I think to myself.

The guards seem convinced by our papers and by Nate's "Greek." They nod at us and wave us on. The fellow in the truck calls *shalom* to us, Hebrew for "hello, goodbye, and peace," and we all shout shalom back. I feel quite impressed that we've pulled this off.

As we reach the truck our new guide shakes hands with Miriam and Nate and congratulates them. "*Mazel tov,*" he says. Miriam very nicely motions to me and makes sure I get a lot of the credit.

"I'm sorry," says our driver, "I assumed you were one of the children."

"Hardly," Nate remarks. "She single-handedly saved me from being arrested."

The driver shakes my hand then too, and indicates that the quicker we are on our way the better. In fact the Polish guards, still drunk, have started screaming at us and pointing their weapons. It looks like they are quite capable of shooting at us *over* the border. We scramble into the back of the truck, which screeches away the minute we are all seated.

It's a short trip to Nachod, the small Czech town near the border, and once we arrive we are taken directly to a Red Cross processing center. People are streaming in and out of the building—even at this early hour. We're taken to a large room where we are examined by a group of doctors and nurses. There's no privacy as they prod and poke us, listening to our lungs to make sure we don't have T.B. and checking us for infectious diseases like typhus, or measles, or fevers.

I notice that they make the men take off their shirts and they check them carefully—especially under the arms. Just ahead of me a man is being checked when the doctor barks in Yiddish, "So now you're pretending to be a Jew. I thought we were worse than dogs, only vermin." Then the doctor switches to German. "You can never pay for what you've done but you won't escape this way."

The man looks around frantically.

I, and everyone else in that room, know what the doctor has found—the tattoo every S.S. guard has, just under the armpit. He is a Nazi.

My stomach sinks. Somehow I fully expect him to pull a machine gun out of the air and to mow us all down. For a minute a feeling of helplessness overwhelms me. After the war ended, when I heard that six million Jews had died, I wondered, did no one fight? Did they just take us all like lambs to the slaughter? But we *did* fight in many ghettos. And we organized resistance activities even in the camps. But the horrible truth was they had guns and if you tried to fight a Nazi with a gun and all you had was your bare hands, you were killed. And then, we were so naive. When they rounded us up did it ever occur to *anyone* that they would shoot us? Or gas us? Not at first. They did things no one ever could have imagined. That was our trouble. We couldn't imagine an evil big enough. But now I can.

A murmur rises in the room. I have the overwhelming desire to go and rip him up, limb from limb. Quickly, two of the Red Cross authorities grab him and pull him out of the room, before any of us can do anything.

I am declared fit, as are all the children. We're given breakfast, then packed off to the train station where we are put on an old rickety train and begin our trip to Bratislava in southeastern Czechoslovakia. From there we are to go to the border and try to get into Austria.

Leah sits beside me in the compartment. Across from us sits a young boy, one of the kids who'd also lived in the forest. He is, perhaps, twelve. His eyes sparkle as the train moves out of the station. He claps his hands in glee.

"We're out of Poland!" he exclaims. "We'll never have to go back there again!"

"Goodbye, graveyard," cries a thin, pale girl. "Every step I took I walked on a dead body."

Three million Jews from Poland had died. Entire towns of ten thousand, twenty thousand, fifty thousand Jews were left with one or two or fifty. She is right. Poland is a graveyard.

Then this girl whose name is Sima begins to sing. She has the most beautiful voice. It's clear and sweet. She sings songs of Shabbat, of life in the towns and villages. And then she sings a song which describes a person who dreams she wakes up in a land of palaces with silver doors, gardens with trees, birds singing. But the dreamer wakes in a concentration camp and the chorus goes:

> *It is a lie*
> *It is a lie*
> *It is a useless dream*
> *There is no palace in the desert, no*
>   *field, no trees.*

Some of the children begin to cry. They sob, both young and old, and they comfort one another, crying in their arms.

Leah takes my hand.

"I never cry," she says.

"Me neither," I agree. Although something inside me feels like breaking, wants to break—but I won't let it. Too dangerous. More dangerous than running across a border with bullets at your back.

I stood on a box in the factory, making bullets for the German Army, bullets that would kill my cousins, my friends. I had had friends in Kurov, Rochelle especially, who was a tomboy and who played sports and climbed trees and who wasn't afraid of anything. The older women put me on a box so when the commander walked through I looked old enough to be working. After all, if you couldn't work you went straight to the gas. And they hid me when the selections came at the camp. They hid me under one of the bunks and threw rags over me.

I used to mutter and curse as I made the bullets. One day the Polish kapo asked me why. I told her. She showed me how to make the casings so the bullets would misfire. And then I felt much better about my work.

The trip takes us a full twenty-four hours. The train stops every fifteen or twenty minutes at each little hamlet and town on the way. There are other refugees on the train of course, not just us. In fact the train is crammed full of Jews who have managed to get over the border to Nachod. At the Red Cross station a worker said thousands were crossing at various points every day. So many, in fact, that the Polish government was actually having discussions with the Jewish Agency about making it unofficially legal to leave Poland. The British would hate that, of course. They don't want any country to make it easy for the Jews to leave—that would mean more trying to get into Palestine.

When the train stops at a crossing we see passengers from trains returning to Poland with Poles who have been in camps. Sometimes we pass trains going in the opposite direction to Germany, full of Poles who had collaborated with the Germans and who have been kicked out of Poland. These Poles are of German descent, and had become powerful during the war. Now they are going "home" to a Germany most of them have never seen. I find them so disgusting I can hardly look at them.

We feed the children thick slices of bread rubbed with garlic and salt, and somehow Nate has managed to get some sausage, which he divides between us. As night draws down and the children begin to fall asleep I watch as we pass under the yellow lamps of the train station and people get on or off the train, looking in the night like the ghosts from my stories.

Finally, at five-thirty in the morning, the train pulls into Bratislava. We are met by an older woman. She leads us through streets with massive stone buildings on either side. I see a funny shaped church with a round bulb on top which looks just like an onion. We reach the market square which is busy, peasants setting up stands of red cherries, white radishes, green peppers, yellow onions, cheeses, and flowers. My mouth waters. And then I realize that Leah, my little friend, has grabbed a handful of cherries from a stand and has stuffed them in her pockets.

A young man, the owner of the stand, starts to scream, I suppose it's Czech, "thief" or something like that. My first instinct is to run, so I grab Leah's hand. They might shoot us or at the very least put Leah in jail. We need to escape. I break out in a sweat as more peasants scream and yell.

Then, suddenly, our new guide is paying the young man and talking to him and everyone is nodding and smiling. She buys some radishes too and gives them to me to carry and some onions, which she gives to Sima, until all the peasants are smiling and nodding to one another.

To Nate and Miriam she says, "I told him that I'd asked the child to pick up some fruit for our breakfast."

Nate walks over to us and says to Leah, "Why did you do that?"

"I was hungry," she answers, simply.

He looks very sad for a moment and then says, "Of course you were. But you don't have to steal anymore."

She gazes at him skeptically, thinking perhaps he is joking with her.

"We'll always make sure you have food," he reassures her.

She looks up at me.

"Is that true?"

I can't answer at first. Nate watches me, wanting me to back him up, to teach her that stealing is wrong. But is it? Hasn't it kept her alive when *no one* would feed or help a little innocent child? What if she needs to do it again? Is the world suddenly a safe place? I don't think so.

"I'm not sure," I answer finally.

Leah nods in satisfaction. "*You* tell me when you are," she says.

I can hardly look at Nate. I know he's disappointed in me. But he says nothing.

"Come children," he says, smiling, "we'll all go and have some breakfast."

Chapter 6

We arrive at an old stone building which certainly looks as if it has seen better days.

"The Hotel Jolen," the old woman declares. "This is where UNRRA has set up a center for refugees." I know that UNRRA is the United Nations organization which takes care of displaced persons.

There is a gaping hole on one side of the roof where the hotel has been bombed. The windows overlooking the street are cracked and thick with dirt. We walk through a small door cut into a large wooden entrance—probably used for horse and carriage by some wealthy nobleman a long time ago. We enter a big filthy courtyard, old horse dung in piles on the pavement. To one side is a stone staircase which spirals up to the other floors. We trudge up the stairs to the reception room on the second floor. Beside the reception room is another room with a few beds and mattresses. The walls are bare of wallpaper and water stained but they are not bare. They are covered in writing—names of refugees who had passed through the center and scrawled on the stairwells and walls. Beside their names are written the towns they came from. Soon everyone who can read is reading and the older children are reading out loud to the younger ones.

My heart is starting to pound again. I hate it! There is no point getting excited. No point having any hope. Still, I read every single name, then I read them again out loud for Leah, who can read a bit after her months in the kibbutz but finds the rough scrawls almost impossible to decipher.

Suddenly, as I am reading out the names, Leah catches her breath. "What did you say?"

I repeat the last name.

"No, not that one. The one before."

"Sayde Leifman. Lublin."

"That's my aunt," Leah whispers. "My Auntie Sayde. My mother's sister." Her eyes are filling up with tears.

"Look," I point, "there's a date here. Leah, she was here only about a week ago. Maybe we'll find her. Maybe we'll catch up with her."

Leah looks at me. "She could be my mother," she says quietly.

"Yes," I say, giving her a hug. "She could. And we'll find her."

I take Leah to the reception room and have the officials there look in their records. They say that Sayde left for Vienna just yesterday and that they are planning to send us there tomorrow.

They feed us white radishes and sour cream, rye bread and real butter, and, of course, Leah shares her few cherries with everyone. I haven't tasted fresh fruit in six years. It is like eating a little present straight from paradise.

We stay at the hotel for all of that day, reading and rereading the names, taking care of the children, meeting others who are also on their way to Vienna. That night we sleep on the floors, the next morning get up early, and are taken to the station. We are put on a special UNRRA train with about 200 other refugees, most of them young *chalutzim*, which is Hebrew for "pioneers," like Nate and Miriam who have been training in kibbutzim in Poland or Hungary or Czechoslovakia. They are in high spirits, they chat and talk to one another, in Hebrew of course, as we are all still supposed to be Greeks. I wonder how they can be so happy after what they've been through. I feel older than all of them, and like an outsider. Still, Leah keeps hold of my hand as if she, at least, needs me.

A Brichah worker introduces himself and tells us he'll be in charge of this huge trainload of Jews and of trying to get us all across the border. The train trip only lasts about three quarters of an hour. We get off at a small station and the Brichah man leads us out of the station by a side gate. We march down a dusty road, the hot midday sun beating down on our heads. Nate and Miriam walk at the head of our little group, Leah and I at the end, but we are only a small part of a huge mass of trudging people all walking two by two—mothers with babies, teenagers, a few old people. It is rare even to see anyone over the age of thirty-five. Most died, the young had a better chance to survive. Everyone carries knapsacks, or old suitcases, or burlap bags, and some have their few possessions in paper bags. We each have two loaves of bread attached by string slung over our shoulders, our ration from the Hotel Jolen. After a while the older ones start to carry the little ones, who can't walk any farther in the hot sun.

The only sound that can be heard are the ground crunching under our feet and the geese honking at us as we pass them on the road. I am wearing a skirt, blouse, tights, and shoes as well as a heavy sweater, because I'd heard that sometimes they take your belongings at the border, unless you are actually wearing them. In fact most people have on heavy coats and everyone pours with sweat. I carry a little four-year-old on my back.

We walk through a village where people stare placidly at us except for a young girl who runs up to the line and offers some of us water from the town well.

We marched in columns two by two away from Auschwitz. It was cold, there was snow on the ground, and all I had on my feet were wooden clogs which bit and blistered and the thin dress I'd been wearing since I got to the camp. We marched and marched, only the sound of our footsteps in the snow and the shots as someone fell. If you even stumbled you were shot. So I concentrated on putting one foot in front of the other, pick up one foot, put it down, pick it up, put it down. . . .

Saul tricked me. There is always time to remember.

We walk over a stone causeway and arrive at the border. Three Czech guards look at us without any comment. The Brichah worker begins to call out names. As he calls a person's name they run across the border. Since the names are Cohen, Rosenburg, Leipsig, etc., they are obviously not Greek and the guards seem well aware of that. In fact the guards chuckle as, one by one, we hurry over the border into Austria.

Austria is split into different zones, and we are now in the Russian zone. We have to get to the U.S. zone where Jewish refugees are treated like people and given freedom. We can't see any Russians at the border, so once the Czechs have let us through we appear to be home free. We continue to march along. We do eventually walk past some Russian soldiers playing soccer, but no one stops us. Finally, hot, exhausted, but relieved, we reach a small train station. Our Brichah leader hurries us into the third-class carriages, and we are on our way to Vienna. It is around four P.M.

In about an hour we change trains and no longer have the compartments to ourselves. The train is stuffed to overflowing and I feel myself begin to get short of breath. Suddenly someone takes my hand. Leah is holding the other one so she follows as a matter of course. I recognize a kid from our group, one of the older ones, a boy. He leads me over the bags and scrambles onto the roof of the train. I gladly follow, Leah close behind.

"As long as we lie flat, we'll be fine." He grins.

He is quite nice looking, medium height, high cheekbones, high forehead, large brown eyes, and black wavy hair. He wears a small round pair of glasses.

"My name is Zvi," he says. "And you are Ruth. You looked like you were having trouble catching your breath."

"I was," I admit. "Thank you, this is much better."

"How old are you, Ruth?" he asks.

"Seventeen," I answer.

He looks at me skeptically.

"And you?" I ask.

"Almost sixteen."

He is actually a year older than I, but is considered one of the babies. Well, that is *his* fault. He should have realized he'd be treated like a baby if he told the truth.

"It's hard to believe we're on our way," he sighs. "I've dreamed of this every day since I was a little kid. And I vowed if I made it through the war, I'd go to Palestine and build a Jewish homeland where no one could ever hurt us again!"

"Oh, please!" I snap, absolutely sick of this starry-eyed stuff, everyone spouting the same thing over and over again.

"Don't you want to go?" he asks.

The wind blows against my face, cooling me off for the first time that day.

"This wind feels good," I say to him. "That's what

I know now. Maybe that's all I'll ever know."

"Then why are you here?" He seems bewildered.

"Because they asked me," I explain. "Because I had nothing better to do."

"You're making this incredibly dangerous trip over half a continent because you had *nothing better to do*?" His voice is incredulous. "It's dangerous. We could be caught. Killed. The worst is yet to come!"

"I wasn't exactly safe in Poland," I reply.

"No," he agrees and then gives me an intense look.

"They took away everything from you, Ruth," he says. "Don't let them take your heart as well."

"What heart?" I say.

He puts his hand on my chest, just above my breast. And he looks into my eyes.

"This one," he whispers. "You still have it, but it's been frozen. Maybe the heat of the desert in Palestine will thaw it."

His hand is hot on my chest, his eyes burn into me. I feel a bit dizzy.

He drops his hand.

"You know we're on our way to the famous Rothschild Hospital in Vienna?" he says.

I nod.

"So have you heard the jokes they used to tell about the Rothschilds?"

"Some," I say. The Rothschilds were one of the few really rich Jewish families in Europe, so jokes about them were everywhere.

My father sat at the head of the Sabbath table. Everyone was laughing. Our guest from out of town was telling jokes.

"A schnorrer, or 'beggar,' tells his friend, 'If I were a Rothschild, I'd be richer than a Rothschild.'

"'How can that be?' asks his friend.

"'Simple—I'd do a little teaching on the side.'"

And then Father said, "I have one. Rothschild stopped at a little inn on his way to Vienna and ordered eggs for breakfast. When he'd finished, the waiter brought him the bill—thirty rubles.

"'Thirty rubles for a few eggs,' Rothschild cried. "'Impossible! Are eggs so scarce around here?'

"'No,' said the waiter. 'But Rothschilds are!'"

I'd forgotten how there was always laughter at our home.

Zvi starts to tell a Rothschild joke.

"A schnorrer wrangled an appointment with Rothschild by insisting he had a foolproof way for the banker to make half a million rubles.

"'So, let's hear this great idea of yours,' said Rothschild.

"'Simple,' said the schnorrer. 'When your daughter marries you are going to give her a dowry of a million rubles, yes?'

"'Yes.'

"'So I'm here to tell you that I'll marry her for half that!'"

Leah giggles. It's the first time I've seen her laugh

at all. Even I feel the corners of my mouth turn up a bit.

Zvi regales us with little jokes and comic sketches until it is time to go inside. It is dusk when we get off the train and follow our Brichah guide onto two trolley cars which are linked together. These take us through Vienna to the Rothschild Hospital in the U.S. zone. When we get to the hospital the entrance is crammed with people awaiting our arrival. Hundreds line the sidewalk leading up to central doorways, cheering us, waiting to see if there are any friends or relatives in our group.

I look, despite myself, as people around me exclaim and cry as they find someone. And then, suddenly, Leah drops my hand and a woman is standing over her crying, "Leahle, my little Leahle, is it you? You look just like your mother." And Leah, who never cries, throws her arms around her auntie and weeps.

I go in alone, for there is no one for me, but I don't care, I tell myself; I'd expected no one.

Chapter 7

The Rothschild Hospital is packed with Jewish refugees from Poland, like me, and others from Yugoslavia, Greece, Romania, Hungary, Slovakia. As I walk down the corridors there is a babble of strange and different languages although it seems the most common is Yiddish—even that in various dialects.

Our group follows the Brichah guide down a staircase into the basement. We pass some large rooms where classes are being conducted and are taken to a room where we undergo yet another medical exam. Surely by now they must have examined us enough! The lines are long and the children are tired and cranky.

After I am examined, *again,* I am given a form to fill out.

Army D.P. registration forms.

Claimed Nationality—*Polish*

Last Permanent Residence or Residence as of Jan. 1, 1938—*Kurov, Poland*

Desired Destination—*Germany* (We can't officially tell the truth about where we're going.)

Usual Trades, Occupation or Profession—(I'm tempted to put down "child" but I leave that blank.)

Languages Spoken in Order of Fluency—*Polish, Yiddish, Hebrew, German*

A young bleary-eyed worker hands me my own I.D. card and tells me that I can now travel anywhere in the U.S. occupied zone of Vienna. I am a person now, with an identity.

Nate, Miriam, and I get the children settled in an upstairs ward packed with beds. Nate goes to speak to the Brichah representatives, to try to convince them to send these children on to Italy quickly. This is no place for them and Nate has heard that there are now special children's camps set up—some in Austria, some in Italy.

We decide we might as well use our freedom, so on our second day we take the children on an outing, tourists in Vienna. I'd heard travelers at our house speak of Vienna, of course, how beautiful it was, how grand, how elegant, but today everything looks dilapidated and dirty, and the supposedly grand buildings that still stand and haven't been bombed have little effect on me. The children seem to feel the same— after what we've all been through, trying to act like we're on holiday feels hollow.

Zvi tags along beside me everywhere, constantly telling jokes and making the children laugh. On the third day after our arrival he takes me to the opera. I don't even really know what the opera is, but the Jewish Agency has given us money for movies and theater and Zvi convinces me to go. The voices are quite beautiful but everyone stares at us in our shabby clothes as though we're from another planet. Of course I know that in a way we are.

We've been here a week when they move us to barracks in a huge displaced persons camp, where people wait to be sent legally to other D.P. camps in Germany, or farther on, illegally to Italy. We're supplied food, clothes, and necessities by what we call the "Joint," the American Jewish Joint Distribution Committee. I am pretty amazed by what I find in this camp. There are at least five thousand Jews, most of them young. They have organized themselves into different kibbutzim and attend classes in Hebrew, history, and Bible studies. They also have classes for all the different skills one might need for a kibbutz life in Palestine. It becomes clear to me that this yearning for Eretz Israel is a serious business. These people are going there. Nothing is going to stop them. A tiny little part of me wakes up and takes notice. Because I'm going too, aren't I? Or do I want to go to Germany and a camp there? Or back "home"?

I sit on my bunk and stare at the kids, at workers running in and out, at the excitement on people's faces. I want someone to pinch me so I can feel *something, anything*. I'm sick of this numbness, of feeling so alone and outside of everything, but I know it's too dangerous to wake up. Also, although I hate to admit it, I miss Leah. Which just proves that I shouldn't allow myself to become attached to anyone.

Zvi comes into the room and sits down beside me.

"If you tell me another joke," I warn him, "I'll kill you. I'm not in the mood."

"I've just heard that the British are really cracking down on ships going to Palestine," Zvi says glumly. "Even if they send us straight on to Italy, and even then if we can get on a boat, we'll be stopped at the three-mile limit, just as we see Palestine, and boarded by the British, and taken away to a detention camp."

He sighs. For a minute I think the impossible has happened and that Zvi is actually discouraged.

"Never mind," he says, brightening, "at least we'll be in Palestine. And who knows, maybe we'll be the lucky ones and escape their boats."

"Lucky, sure," I snort. "We Jews are just full of luck."

"Which reminds me," says Zvi, ignoring my threat, "two Jews sat in a coffeehouse, discussing the fate of their people.

"One said, 'How miserable is our lot. Pogroms, plagues, quotas, discrimination, Hitler—sometimes I think we'd be better off if we'd never been born.'

"'Sure,' said the other. 'But who has that much luck—maybe one in fifty thousand?'"

Zvi grins at me and before I can stop myself, a small giggle escapes me.

He winks at me. "This one you find funny?"

"In a sick sort of way," I reply.

"Ah, you like the darker jokes," Zvi says. "I have another."

"An Austrian Jew, just realizing Hitler is about to take over the country, goes to a travel agent who takes out a globe and begins to go over various possibilities. But then, like now, each country had a different excuse for not taking in any Jews. One by one each country on the globe was eliminated as a possible place to go to. Finally, in desperation the Jew asks, 'Haven't you got another globe?' "

I give him a slow smile. "That's just the way I feel. No one wants us, especially our own countries, and now the British won't let us into Palestine. Why won't they? Don't they see what we've been through?"

"Britain doesn't really care about us," Zvi explains. "They care about Russia moving in everywhere, and the threat of Communism, and about Berlin and about India—we're just a little sideshow. Maybe if last winter hadn't been so bad things would be different."

"Are you telling me they're closing Palestine to us because of the weather?" I ask, incredulous.

"In a way," Zvi replies. "In England they had no fuel for their trucks, which they needed to transport coal for heating. They were cold and miserable and couldn't afford to make the Arabs mad—since the Arabs have all the oil."

I roll my eyes.

"Don't worry, it doesn't matter," Zvi says. "We'll

get to Palestine no matter what. Can you imagine what it will be like to be in a country where the Jews make the laws, run the schools, run the courts? Can you even imagine? No more laws like in Poland where Jews can't own this, Jews can't be elected here, Jews can't join that. Never again!"

I have to admit it's an appealing thought.

Just then Miriam comes in.

"Get your stuff together," she announces. "We're leaving!"

"We are?" I'm really surprised. "But they just brought us here."

"We're going to try to cross the border with a group of chalutzim," she explains. "And they're leaving *now*."

Quickly we gather the kids together.

"You see," Zvi says, "we're on our way!"

Outside a line of trucks painted with big Red Cross symbols stands waiting, people piling in.

The trucks take us to a small train station and there we're settled on a train. As soon as the train begins to move so do all the young people we're traveling with—they all start to dance! The chalutzim, the children grabbed between them, dance the hora in lines up and down the train. Soon even the saddest of the children is dancing and singing—even me. They won't take no for an answer and pull us all along with them. They are celebrating the fact that they are finally on their way to Italy, and that can mean only one thing— a boat to Palestine!

Near the end of the day, the train stops close to Innsbruck and we are taken by truck to an old abandoned army barracks near Saalfelden.

When it is dark an Austrian guide and a new Brichah leader, Uri, take us over the Alps. It's been raining all day and the climb is miserable as we slog through mud and try to haul ourselves and our luggage (I only have a knapsack so it's easier for me) *and* the children through the soggy forest. Still, no one complains, including the children. I begin to be rather impressed with my fellow travelers. They are incredibly brave and well disciplined and always ready to help one another. We run into some trouble when we reach a fast-running mountain stream. Some of the younger girls are afraid to wade through it and won't budge. I don't care—after all, what have I got to lose? But these girls are genuinely panic-stricken. Nate and a bunch of fellows his age decide to lay face down in the water so the girls can walk on their backs over the water. When it's all over they have nothing to dry themselves with and have to make the rest of the trip sopping wet. Zvi trudges beside me, his clothes almost freezing on him, but he honestly doesn't seem to mind. It's a long hard walk for everyone. We often have to carry the children and a couple of times people get so tired they sit down and refuse to go on. Others pick them up and almost carry them—no one will be left behind. We hike all night and just as dawn breaks we come out right near the border. The first thing we see is a battalion of French soldiers. We must be in the French occupied zone of Austria. The soldiers don't look too happy to see us. Their commander asks us who we are and Uri shows our fake Greek papers. This doesn't wash. The commander knows quite well who we are and phones for trucks to come and return us to the D.P. camps.

Nate and Uri whisper to each other, then Nate spreads the word to get all the women and children out of the way. We hurry the children over to an old barn not far away, then watch as the two groups stand and face each other. I can't hear what they are saying but obviously our guys refuse to move. I can see the French commander getting madder and madder until finally he orders his troops forward to break up this little demonstration. As soon as they move, so do our guys, ready to fight.

"I'm not staying here," I declare. But half the women are already ahead of me, running out to the road to join the fight, which is well under way. Many of these women have survived by fighting as partisans against the Nazis and they certainly aren't going to stand by and watch their friends be attacked. I fly out of the barn with them. I throw myself at a smallish soldier who tries to push me away but I give him a solid hit with my fist on his jaw and he goes down—very surprised!

Then a whistle blows and suddenly the soldiers' guns are off their shoulders and we are being hit with rifle butts—one catches me across the shoulder and back and I crash over, onto my own French victim, hitting him again. Soon the scene is a grim one—almost all of us down and bleeding, the French soldiers standing among us looking bewildered and somewhat ashamed. For a few minutes there is complete silence. Then the commander motions Uri and Nate over to him. I am close enough to hear what they say. They all speak German to one another.

"This is terrible," the commander says. "Frankly, I never thought you'd fight. I mean, I never knew Jews could fight. . . ." He gets confused and stops.

"I'm sorry," he mutters. "On second thought your papers seem all right to me. You just be on your way."

"Thank you," Uri says solemnly and shakes the commander's hand.

I look around for Zvi. He is not too far away, a nasty lump on his head. He's searching the ground for his glasses. I find them but they are broken in half.

"I'm blind without them," he groans.

"Still," I say, "I'm sure you'll have a joke about it by tomorrow."

He grins at me as he painfully gets to his feet.

"I hope so," he says, "if my brain is still working then." He looks at me. "Why were you fighting?" he asks. "I thought you didn't care about anything."

I shrug. "I'm not sure myself why I did it. Maybe I couldn't resist the chance to fight back."

"That's the whole point of this trip," Zvi says.

"Going somewhere where no one can bully us."

"Oh, be quiet," I say. "And don't look so smug." He is making me mad, because, frankly, I just surprised myself.

We collect the children. They look terribly anxious, terrified I'm sure, watching their protectors get hurt.

"We're fine," I assure them. "And now we're going to go over the border to Italy!"

The children clap their hands.

Of course, the ordeal is not necessarily over. We can still get stopped by the Italian guards, or police on the other side of the border, and be sent back. But we have a bit of luck. Maybe we're allowed a little now. There are a couple of Italian guards on the border but they just laugh and wave us on. We're across!

Brichah trucks, disguised as British army trucks, are waiting for us on the Italian side. I like that. The British are looking everywhere for us and we are disguising ourselves as them! Even the drivers are dressed in British army uniforms.

We drive through the Italian countryside, deep and lush, the mountains rising up around us, the sky a clear perfect blue, the air smelling of flowers and morning dew, and for one brief minute I feel alive and happy to be alive.

"Aren't you happy to be alive? To have made it?" It was an American soldier trying to cheer me up as I recuperated in the hospital.

"Better people than I died," I answered. "I don't deserve to be here."

"Yes, you do," he said, giving me a piece of chocolate. "You're just my daughter's age. Does that mean she doesn't deserve to live either?"

I think about that as I settle down into the truck and we are driven to our first stop on the way to the children's camps.

Chapter 8

Italy in July is simply breathtaking in its beauty. I feel myself on the verge of tears as we travel, first to Merano to be processed and from there, with Nate, Miriam, and our group of twenty children, on to a children's camp in the mountains of Northern Italy. It makes me want to cry because it's so pretty—the lakes, the deep green forests, the flowers, the hills and mountains, and that deep blue sky—but I know that the human beings inhabiting it are often ugly. We don't deserve this planet.

Zvi is keeping the little children occupied playing games with them as we drive, Nate and Miriam gaze around as I do, but their eyes are gleaming . . . they are full of hope. We arrive at a beautiful old villa tucked into the hills, and as the children clamber out of the truck, other children pour out of the house to welcome us. They clap and offer us each a chocolate wrapped in silver foil as a little gift. Seeing everyone together like that I suddenly notice that the way the kids are behaving seems to have a lot to do with their age.

The youngest seem quite happy as long as they are with someone, holding a hand or being taken care of, but the minute they are on their own they grow quiet and fearful. They rarely cry of course because they had been trained not to—crying was almost always dangerous and could give you away. The older ones, young adults in their twenties, like Nate and Miriam, are full of energy. And then the kids my age—for the most part I realize that they are a lot like me. Miserable. In fact, outside of Zvi who is so outgoing, and really more like the older Chalutzim, it occurs to me that I've barely gotten to know anyone of our group. There are four others around my age and none of us bothers with more than a "hello, how are you?", that sort of thing. Three are girls, one is a boy.

A little child drops his candy, and another one picks it up and stuffs it in his pocket. Even the littlest ones are still trying to survive.

The head of the camp, a tall man, balding on top with square black glasses and a round face, claps his hands and starts to make a little speech.

"Shalom," he says, speaking in Hebrew. "Hello, children. My name is Mayer. We are so happy that you've come to stay with us. While you're here you're going to be very busy. Everyone will go to school, will help with the chores, and everyone will learn what they need to so they can be good citizens in Eretz Israel, the land of Israel.

"Any child over the age of fifteen will be a youth leader and should come to the central meeting room after dinner for a briefing on your job.

"Now you must all be hungry. So let's go eat!"

The children follow him into the villa to a central

dining room where a hot stew of potatoes and meat and carrots and onions is handed out. We're given fresh bread and the water tastes funny, full of minerals from the well, but I like it.

The villa is very pretty with high roofs and lots of rooms and bedrooms and after dinner, once we settle the little ones, we walk into a meeting room which adjoins the dining room. We are introduced to one another and I register the names of the others in my group for the first time—Rivka, Fanny, Sima, Karl. I wonder at the fact that I haven't even noted their names before this—I really have been sleepwalking. There are about fifty other kids our age there, who have obviously been at the camp for awhile.

We are told that it will be our job to help make the children better. (And who will make us better, I wonder?)

We are to take turns teaching. Teaching, I think, that's funny. I have a grade four education, I was ten when I was taken away. I was just starting grade five that fall of 1939.

Joshua, my oldest brother, had decided to take action. Only the day before Simon had been beaten up by some kids from school who'd called him a filthy Jew pig and thrown cow manure at him from the side of the road. Joshua was not big and tough so he made a deal with some big tough Polish boys. They would be our bodyguards. If anyone beat us up, they'd have to answer to them! And it had worked. That day we walked home from school with no threats. But the next day the Nazis came and Jew beating became legal.

I guess a few of us must have skeptical looks on our faces, so Mayer clarifies his remarks. "You will *help* the teachers I've brought in and run your own classes when possible." He pauses. "Can any of you remember how to play games?"

A few hands go up. Games, I think, I used to play games, didn't I? Of course, I'd had dolls and we'd skipped rope, we'd played house. Tentatively, I put up my hand.

"Of course you remember." Mayer smiles. "But the little ones never learned how to play. They have nothing to remember. So perhaps you new arrivals can help our other youth leaders to teach them to play.

"And we'll be going on hikes outside because fresh air and sunshine is good for everyone, we'll even hike into the mountains some days. We have intensive Hebrew classes and Jewish history classes and even some Torah study for those who want it. The little ones always like the Bible stories.

"Now we already have a lot going on here, so for you new arrivals, just try to fit in as best you can. There's lots of work to be done. Oh, yes, one last thing. I want each of you to pick at least five children and encourage them to tell you their stories. We want every single story—what happened to them during the war—written down. It'll help the children to talk, and also, we want a record."

I don't want to do that. I don't really want to hear what they've been through. But I decide not to say anything. Maybe no one will notice that I'm not participating.

Finally, we are all sent off to bed. I'm assigned to a large dorm, with kids around my age. Although I'm sticking to my seventeen years old story, here it doesn't seem to matter, everyone in my group is around fifteen to seventeen and no one seems to care if you are one or the other. I suppose they realize that we are all very old people by now, so a few years either way makes no difference. Zvi makes sure he has the bunk on one side of me, Rivka is on the bunk on my other side. She has flame-red hair, her face is covered with freckles, and she is terribly thin, still looking like she's just come out of a concentration camp. As we lie in bed she starts to talk to me. She asks me where I grew up and I tell her.

"I'm from Warsaw," she says in Polish. "I was in the ghetto there."

"Were you one of the fighters?" I ask. Jews had fought the Nazis in Warsaw and although they'd lost—how can a few guns compete with tanks?—they had caused the Nazis lots of trouble.

"Yes," she says. "And then I escaped to the woods and fought with the Polish partisans."

"I thought you'd been in a camp," I say, and then realize I might have hurt her feelings.

"Because I'm so thin," she nods. She sighs. "I can't

eat. I went for a year and a half on almost nothing and now I can't eat. I put a little bite in my mouth and I feel like throwing it up."

"What you need," I say, "is some of my mother's chicken soup."

Mother was considered one of the best cooks in all of Kurov. Of course we were lucky because with the store we had fresh food and lots of it. There was always a soup on the stove—vegetable, or chicken, or a beet borscht. After school she would have fresh cake for us covered in sweet crumbs, or blueberry muffins. On Friday she'd make fresh challah, fish, farfel with liver and onions. In season we'd eat cherries, plums, and gooseberries. At Shuvuot she'd make cheesecake; for Rosh Hashanah, apple cake; for Purim, strudel; for Hanukkah, my favorite, fresh cake donuts with sugar and jam inside; for Passover, sponge cake.

Father woke up every morning at four A.M. and put sawdust on the floor and then at six, the baker came with fresh bread and the farmers came with eggs and vegetables. At nine, Father sat down for a breakfast of thick fresh bread with onions and salt dipped in oil. And sometimes a herring.

I hadn't had these thoughts in years. I know a lot of people in the camps dreamed of food and had visions of food all the time, but I made myself forget it. Early on, when I realized I would always be hungry, always yearning for food, I told myself that the only thing to do was forget that it had ever existed. All that existed then was the crust of hard bread or watery soup made of nettles. And I never expected more.

"You'll get very sick if you don't eat," I say to Rivka.

"I know," she replies, "but I don't know how to start eating again."

"You don't think you deserve it," I say, "because your family died."

And suddenly I know I am talking about myself.

"That's right," she whispers, surprised I understand so well.

I look into her eyes. "I know how you feel."

She nods, then lies down to sleep. I turn my head and look at Zvi. He shakes his head, then reaches over and touches my arm, where my tattoo is.

"You deserve everything good in the world," he murmurs.

I smile.

His eyes open wide. "You smiled! I've never seen you smile. What did I say!"

"You're so funny," I whisper. "There *is* no good in the world. You just have no idea!"

He grows angry then. It's the first time I've seen him mad. "Don't tell me I have no idea," he says. "Don't tell me that."

I could kick myself. I don't know what happened to him and his family but it's bound to be horrible.

"I'm sorry," I apologize, and I really mean it. "Please forgive me."

He nods but still looks shaken.

"It's all right," he says. Then he pauses. "My pain is no less than yours, Ruth."

I touch his hand, which is clenched on the bed. "I know. I know that."

I have a hard time getting to sleep—the strange room, all the new faces, and so many crying out, or weeping, or moaning as they sleep. I finally drop off but wake the next morning exhausted. My dreams were worse than usual, bodies in flames, the smell of burning flesh. Still, I have no time to feel sorry for myself. We are all put to work at once—either taking classes in Hebrew or history, or giving classes.

I am put in charge of a group of ten children for playtime. They all stare at me expectantly. I rack my brain until I remember one of the first games I'd played, and a game the children should be very good at—hide and seek. When I explain it to them though, some of them become very upset.

"I don't want to hide any more."

"I can't find my mommy."

And so on.

I try to calm them down and think of something a little less threatening. Suddenly I remember the game of tag.

I take them all outside and I say, "I'm it!" And I chase a little boy and tag him. "Now you're it," I say.

He looks at me bewildered. "And what do I do?" he asks.

"Now you have to tag one of the other children but

they must run away so you can't catch them."

"That's mean," a little girl with black curly hair objects.

"It's not mean," I explain, "it's a game. We all run around and get lots of exercise and try not to be it!"

He marches up and tags the little girl with the black curls. "Meany," she screams. "Meany, meany," she starts to cry.

"Wait, wait," I shout. "Look, I have an idea. I'm a Big Bad Monster and if you tag me I'll die so everyone has to try to tag *me*."

This seems to catch their attention. Big people often had been monsters to them. They throw themselves into this game with relish, screaming with delight every time I fall down in a death agony. Some even laugh. That's a lovely sound. Strange, but lovely.

Chapter 9

We've been here almost two weeks now.

Mayer calls me away from my group as we're playing outside. We sit on a flat rock, which overlooks a green valley and a sparkling blue lake.

"Ruth," he says, "you've done a terrific job getting the children to play."

"Thanks," I say, feeling—almost proud of myself, I suppose. "At first they wouldn't do anything. Now they're playing tag, the real way, and we play house except they always end up hiding, and today I'm going to try to teach them some new songs."

"But you haven't done the histories yet," he observes.

"No," I admit.

He looks at me.

"I don't want to," I say. "I really don't want to hear it."

"Have you ever told anyone what happened to you, Ruth?" he says gently.

"There's no point," I reply. "Telling it won't change what happened."

"That's true," Mayer agrees. "But perhaps it'll help you live with it better."

"It won't," I say, getting really angry. "Why should

it? Will saying it out loud bring back my family? Wipe out everything I've seen? Tell me why I'm here at all?"

"Ruth, it won't do any of those things. But maybe it'll make room for memories that aren't all bad. Memories of your family and friends."

"Those hurt too," I say bitterly.

"Well then, Ruth, do it for another reason."

"What?" I answer, sullen, staring at the ground.

"For a record. So the rest of the world can never say it didn't happen." And now *his* voice is fierce, and angry, too.

He's surprised me. I stop for a minute to think.

"That's a good reason," I say finally. And then I realize he too must have a story, must have lost relatives, may have been in the camps. I nod.

During Hebrew class in the afternoon I take Sarah outside onto the same rock. I settle myself with a pen and paper. Sarah is ten years old, originally from Lvov, Poland.

"Sarah," I say, "you know Mayer wants us all to tell our stories, don't you?"

She nods her head.

"I mean, what happened to you in the war."

She nods again.

"Will you tell me?"

"Daddy used to hide us in a kind of closet," she says. "Only it was disguised."

"Was this right at the beginning of the war?" I ask.

"No. First we lived in a big beautiful house. Daddy

was a doctor. He made everyone better. But when the Germans came they put us in a ghetto and took away everything from us. Except Mommy had sewn jewelry and money into our clothes and we wore those to the ghetto so we had money. And my brother Menachim, he had blond hair and blue eyes, so he used to sneak out of the ghetto and use the money to buy us food, because there was no food and we were starving. The Nazis made Mommy and Daddy work in a factory so I had to take care of Moishe, who was only three years old. If the Germans came for a roundup I hid in a closet and I put him in a suitcase."

"Go on."

"He never made a sound," she says proudly, "but I was scared for him."

"Were *you* scared?" I ask.

"Yes. But only when Mommy and Daddy were away. When they were home I knew they'd take care of us."

"And then what do you remember?" I ask. So far, this was a typical story, I thought. I can do this. It'll be O.K.

"One day Daddy said, 'This is it!' The Germans were taking all the Jews out of the ghetto and we knew they would kill us. He had dug a tunnel straight down into the sewer and he made us go down there. The tunnel was dark and scary but he made us.

"Then we were all standing in the sewer and a sewer worker saw us. Daddy told him if he didn't tell on us, Daddy would pay him. The sewer worker said if Daddy paid him lots of money he'd take care of us. So Daddy gave him all our money and the worker, Lopov was his name, got us a couple of boards to put over the water to sleep on. We went into a little side tunnel, you know."

I stare at her. She has black hair and brown eyes, and is very small for her age. Her cheeks are round and her eyelashes long and dark. She recites all this with no emotion, as if she is talking about a walk to the store to buy some milk.

"Then what?" I ask. "How long did you stay there for?"

"We stayed there for a year and a half," she answers.

I gasp.

"And you never went outside?"

"No, but after a few months Mr. Lopov took me down the sewer and showed me the light and told me I *would* get out," she declares. "Because I wouldn't eat or anything. And he brought books so Mommy and Daddy studied with us. We all learned to read and write and we learned the Torah and we learned some maths."

"How did you see?" I ask.

"Oh, we had a lamp." She pauses. "I was very sick I had to go to the bathroom all the time. Everyone did. The water we lived in was sewer water. It smelled awful."

"How did you go to the bathroom?"

"Right there." And then she smiles. "That part was easy 'cause the whole place was a bathroom!

"And then the Russians liberated us," she adds.

"But, what are you doing here?" I ask. "This place is for orphans."

She looks at me a long time before she answers.

"When we got out Mommy was alone one day on the street and some Russian soldiers grabbed her and did bad things to her. I don't know what but she got very sick and Daddy had to take care of her and he couldn't look after us so he sent us to Palestine and when she's better they're going to come, too. Daddy thought we weren't safe in Poland anymore."

I try to speak but my throat is too dry.

"Do you think Mommy will get better?" she asks me.

I take her hand. I clear my throat. "I hope so," I say, "but if she doesn't you'll have to be strong and look after her. All right?"

Sarah thinks about this for a minute.

"I could do that," she says. "I could help Daddy." And her whole face seems to brighten.

"That's right," I say. "And you're lucky your parents are alive," I add.

"I know," she nods. "Sometimes I feel bad because almost everyone here has no parents. Do you have parents?"

Mother and Hannah were frantically trying to

catch a glimpse of me, and Daddy was screaming
"Sayde, Sayde" to my mother as the lines were pushed
away from each other, it was dark, the dogs barked,
people were shoved, the Nazis cursed, a red glow from
the furnaces covered everything. . . .

I never saw them again.

I shake my head, no, pen and paper falling to the
ground.

Sarah takes my hand.

"I could ask Daddy if you could be part of *our* family," she offers.

Tears burn at my eyes but I push them back.

"Thank you," I whisper.

She throws her thin little arms around me and
gives me a hug. "Can I go now?"

I nod, because I can't speak and she runs off back
to her class. I sit there, the sun beating down on me,
for a very long time. I feel fuzzy, my head full of wool.
I can't think, but I can't seem to move either.

Zvi comes out to get me. He picks up the paper
and pen, takes my hand, and leads me into the villa for
some lunch. I eat what he puts in front of me and then
go and lie down on my cot. I fall into a deep, long
sleep and I dream. I dream Mother and Father are
hugging me and kissing me and telling me they love
me. Then Hannah and Joshua are there and they
shower me with hugs and kisses too and tell me to be
brave and to be happy. When I wake up it's almost dinner time and I feel funny. Strange. Like something is

appening inside me but I don't know what.

The next afternoon I have to do another history. This one is with Jonathan, a boy of twelve from Vilna.

"We were always running," Jonathan says, looking at me with his big brown eyes. His curly hair falls over his forehead and as he speaks he often has to push it out of his eyes. "That's what I remember most. And the lice. And . . . and."

I can see he is starting to get upset.

"Let's start at the beginning," I say.

"At first we didn't have to move," says Jonathan, "because we already lived in the Jewish quarter and when the Nazis made a ghetto it was where we lived." He stops.

"Go on," I encourage him.

"So some relatives came to live with us, because no one could live in their houses alone. They were my mother's cousins and I didn't like them. The kids were bratty and cousin Lette smelled real bad and she used to smack me if I did something she didn't like."

"Didn't your mother stop her?"

"She tried, she even told Lette they'd have to leave, but then she didn't have the heart to throw them out. Father had a shoe repair store and he was kept busy doing work for everyone, even for the Nazis, so we had enough food because people would pay us in food—everyone needed shoes.

"Then one day when he was doing work for this Nazi the guy told him he would need the shoes the next day—no later. And Father knew they meant to kill us the next day. Somehow we'd managed to escape the roundups until then. So that night Father took all our money and he bribed a guard and we started to sneak out of the ghetto. There were Father, Mother, my older sister Sarah and the baby, Yahuda. And when we'd gotten a few yards away, I guess just long enough for the guard to put the money away in his pocket, the guard shot at us. Father, Mother, and Sarah were shot so I grabbed Yahuda and ran and we were little and harder to shoot so we escaped. We managed to get into the countryside and finally hid in a barn. And a Polish lady let us stay a few days but soon we had to go and we found another barn and stayed for a bit, and on and on. We traveled at night and if we couldn't stay in a barn we slept outside.

"Some of the Polish peasants used to give me milk for the baby even though we were Jews. And then the baby got sick with a high fever so we hid in a hayloft and I used to sneak down and milk the cow and put a little milk in a can for the baby and for me. And he got better!"

"How old was the baby?" I ask.

"He was eight months old then," he answers. "He would cry and that scared me because that could kill us so I had to hold my hand over his mouth and by the time he was nine months he had learned not to cry."

"How old were you?"

"I was eight."

"You were just a little boy yourself, you did a good job taking care of the baby."

"Finally we had to leave the barn because the farmer found us and he went to report us to the Nazis so we ran into the forest. And that's when I saw . . . I saw . . ."

"What?"

Jonathan shook his head.

"*What*?" Suddenly I feel mean. I'll *make* him tell me. His pain is no worse than mine. He can damn well tell!

"They were lining all the Jews up in the forest," he says, very low, "they were all naked. There was a big pit and an officer went down the row and shot each one in the head and then they fell into the pit. My cousins all died there. My grandparents, too. And all my friends. And their mommies and daddies." He pauses. "And then—just a minute," he says and runs into the villa. In a few minutes he returns pulling Zvi by the hand.

I'm puzzled.

"And then *he* climbed out of the pit," Jonathan says. I stare at Zvi. And I suddenly realize that Zvi has always spent a lot of time with Jonathan, Jonathan looking up to him like an older brother.

"I don't understand," I say, "I thought they shot everyone, one by one."

"They did," Zvi says, "but at the last minute my mother pulled me in front of her and pushed me into the pit, already full of dead bodies. And the Germans didn't notice. I was covered in dead bodies, I had blood all over me, my parents lay beside me, my three older sisters somewhere there too, I was so crushed I couldn't breathe, and then it was over. The Nazis left and I somehow crawled out of the pit. Jonathan and I found the partisans after that. They put the baby in a convent. But this isn't my story. It's Jonathan's."

"But I want you here when I tell it," Jonathan insists.

"All right," Zvi says. "I'll stay, Jonathan."

Jonathan seems to relax a little and then continues. "It was bad at the end when the Germans and Russians were fighting," he says. "We were almost killed lots of times by Russian bombs. But the partisans let me stay with them because of Zvi, because he ran messages for them, and sometimes I would go if there was a place too small for Zvi to crawl through or something. Then when the Russians liberated us I went to find Yahuda but the nuns had given him away for adoption and when we went to get him the family wouldn't give him up but Zvi is going to get him back for me."

"I am," Zvi vows. "I've got Mayer working on it now."

I finish writing and then thank Jonathan. He goes back to class.

"You didn't tell me," I say to Zvi.

"You didn't ask," he replies.

"Zvi, Zvi!!" Mayer is calling. "It's Jonathan."

We run into the main room. Jonathan is throwing

anything he can find—cushions, books, even chairs. He is screaming, hysterically. Zvi runs up to him and grabs him, but Jonathan doesn't even seem to recognize Zvi. Mayer lifts Jonathan in a bear hug and holds him tight so he won't hurt himself.

He flails around desperately for a few more moments then starts to cry uncontrollably and he babbles, "I was little and Mother used to sing to me and read to me and she loved me, she was good and nice, sometimes I was bad and she yelled at me, maybe that's why something bad happened to us and Father always smelt of leather." Then he starts to sob so hard he can't speak and Zvi is trying to hold him and then I start to cry. I sit down right there and I start to cry and I can't stop and it's really quite funny because Zvi doesn't know what to do. He's running back and forth between me and Jonathan, both of us crying, and he's hugging us and he can't be two places at once so finally he drags me over to Jonathan and then he tries to comfort us both, and so does Mayer.

Finally Mayer picks me up and carries me to my cot and Zvi tucks me in and sits and holds my hand and I suppose they put Jonathan to bed, too. The last thing I remember is looking in Zvi's eyes. I think he's crying, too.

Chapter 10

When I wake up it is dark.

I lay on a mound of dead bodies in the camp at Buchenwald and the Nazis began to stick their bayonets into everyone to make sure they were all dead. I was almost dead, but not quite. I'd dragged myself there thinking it was the safest place to be—they wouldn't shoot dead people. I was wrong. Still I was too sick to move, or care, and for some reason I began to say the shema, the way I'd heard others who were about to die say it, "Shema Israel, Adonai Elohanu Adonai, Echad. Hear, O Israel, the Lord our God, the Lord is one." The bayonets missed me altogether. Shortly after, the Americans liberated the camp. As they moved the dead bodies I spoke. The soldier who had grabbed my arm to throw me on the truck yelled in surprise. I was rushed to the hospital. "She's alive!" they yelled. No, I thought, I'm dead. I fought so hard to survive and now I'm dead anyway.

Zvi is asleep at the bottom of my bed. I shake him and wake him up.

"I'm alive," I whisper.

Slowly he leans over and kisses me, full on the mouth.

"So am I," he says in my ear. And then, in an

equally serious tone, "and I'm hungry."

"So am I!" I declare.

We've slept through dinner and now everyone is in the main room, tables pushed back, singing and dancing. We sneak into the kitchen, find some bread and jam, and eat greedily. I feel as though I haven't eaten in years. Then I giggle to myself. I haven't!

Suddenly I feel very shy with Zvi. I've never been kissed before. He stares at me while he eats, a funny look on his face, as if he is embarrassed, too. And of course, the fact that his glasses are taped together in the middle doesn't exactly give him a dignified air. Finally, he can't stand the silence any longer and he grabs my hand.

"Let's dance," he exclaims, and he pulls me into the other room. We join a hora and we whirl around the room and I start to sing, quietly at first, then louder, until I am singing at the top of my lungs. Nate and Miriam come and dance beside me, smiling the whole time as if seeing me dance like this is some kind of miracle.

Maybe it is.

Three weeks after our arrival at the camp, Nate announces to Zvi and me that we'll be leaving at first light the next morning. We are to get the children ready, because we are to board a boat tomorrow night. We hurry and pack the children's gear and then all of us older kids sit in one of the small rooms with Nate and Miriam.

"You'll each take turns with the children," Nate says, "but probably you'll have other responsibilities on the boat as well. For now the most important thing will be to keep them quiet while we're in the truck. We'll be disguised as a British transport, and there'll be boxes at the back in case anyone peeks in. The truck will be covered of course. The British are all over Italy and they are giving the Italians a very hard time—they don't want any of us getting on those boats to Palestine. Oh, and something else you may as well know. Bevin, the British foreign minister, decreed that all refugees caught at sea will no longer be detained in Atlit in Palestine. They are all to be taken to the island of Cyprus and put in camps there."

"No!" Zvi exclaims.

"I'm afraid so." Nate's expression is grim. "I think he believes that we won't try to come if he does that. But he's wrong, isn't he?"

"We've survived Hitler," I scoff. "Does he think *he* can scare us?"

Nate grins at me. "I think he'll soon find that out. It's hard to control people who have nothing to lose.

"When we get to the shore, each of you is to be in command of five children. They must all be lined up in groups of twenty, ready to be ferried out to the boat in dinghies. Again—no noise. Now try to get some sleep."

We go back to our bunks but end up staying up most of the night, sitting on our beds talking. Rivka nibbles on little bits of cheese—Mayer has her on a program where she always has food with her and she has teeny little bites all through the day. It seems to be working. She doesn't look quite so emaciated and her eyes are a little clearer. The rest of us chew on fingernails and try to contain our energy. I'm infected with the general excitement, too. Ever since the day I'd cried I seem to have woken up. I've started to feel things and instead of it being bad and scary, what I've been feeling has been exciting. I've started talking to people and I've made friends with Rivka and Fanny. Fanny is a big girl, almost five ten, and strong. She'd hidden all through war as a Polish farm worker and had had plenty to eat. None of her family had survived, though, so now she wants to go work on a farm in Palestine. Sima is harder to get to know, she's withdrawn, but very artistic. She spends her entire time sketching in pen and ink—chilling drawings of what she's seen. She and I understand each other and will often spend time together just being quiet. Karl is an avid Marxist and spends most of his time trying to convert us to his movement, Borochov. But I'm sticking to Noar Zioni. Rivka belongs to Betar, the right-wing movement, so she and Karl get into terrible arguments all the time.

Zvi stares at me so intensely sometimes that I feel all of me will just melt, right there, into one big puddle. Sometimes I try to make him stop. I put my hands over his eyes but he takes my hands and locks them into his and stares at me some more—in between kisses.

We've only slept a few hours when Nate and Miriam wake us just before dawn. We help the children dress. They are still so sleepy they hardly know what is happening and we hustle them into the dining room for breakfast. We dig into a big breakfast of eggs (from dried egg powder) and bread and jam and then we make sure the children use the bathrooms before we settle them in the truck. We sit among them and wave goodbye to Mayer and the few others who are up that early. And then we are off.

It's a boring ride. Our driver is very strict. No noise. Bathroom breaks by the side of the road last two minutes, no more. We drive all day and it's very hot and uncomfortable but the children are too excited to be put off by a little discomfort. We whisper songs together, play word games, and, of course, Zvi tells jokes. Night falls and still we drive. We feed the children twice— sandwiches which have been made up ahead of time and water, which we all share.

Many of the children finally fall asleep, and I think I've probably dozed a bit too, when I am jolted awake by the truck lurching and jumping.

Some of the children cry out in surprise and we quickly remind them that there can be no noise no matter what. Jonathan is with us, of course, always close to Zvi, and Sarah, and they help us keep the very little ones quiet.

We finally come to a stop and the driver motions for us to get out.

I'm stiff when I jump off the truck into the sand and begin helping the little children down. We are on a beach, with hundreds of other people. Everyone is lined up on the sand in orderly fashion in groups of around twenty. By the shore, teams of men and women are helping the groups into dinghies. Trucks are pulling up behind us for as far as I can see. We must have been driving in a convoy for the last part of the trip.

The children follow us without a peep and we line up behind another group. No one speaks. The only sounds are the trucks pulling up and an occasional command or order to do with the dinghies.

My heart is pounding so loud I am sure Nate will get angry with me for making noise. And then I realize, probably for the very first time, that I really am leaving Europe behind me, Poland behind me, and I'm going somewhere where people just might want me. I know that our truck driver has risked jail for us and that everyone helping here, all the Brichah leaders, are risking their lives for us. It dawns on me that we are important to them—that maybe *I'm* important to them—because of what we've been through and because we are willing to risk our lives to help them make a new country.

We stand for hours in the sand, waiting our turn to get onto the boat. Each group that is put on a dinghy is replaced by another until we get closer and closer to the beach. The water is calm and laps up to the shore, the night warm. Sometimes Zvi stands beside me and holds my hand. Sometimes we have to pick up some little ones, carry them around, soothe them. And finally, it's our turn.

We are helped into a big rubber boat which is attached to the ship by a steel cord. Nate, Miriam, and Fanny move us along by pulling hand over fist on the cord. Slowly we inch out to the boat. A ladder hangs from the massive ship and somehow we have to get the little ones up. We decide who is big enough to go on their own, and they scamper up first. Then we each take a little one and literally put them on the ladder ahead of us, step by step.

I climb up with little Nathan, who is scared but trusts me, and finally he is pulled onto deck and so am I. We are on a big hulking ship but I can't see much. We're hurried down some steps into a deep hold where wooden bunks have been built in three rows, one on top of another. I stop dead. I can't move. It looks exactly like Auschwitz.

Zvi is behind me. "Move, Ruth," he says, "there are a lot of others to board."

"I can't," I say.

"You have to."

"No." I turn and push past him onto the deck. Nate is pulling people off the ladder.

"Let me help," I say to him. "I can't go down there."

"We have to hurry them up," Nate said. "If the

British catch us here in the morning, this boat won't get out to sea."

No one is *ever* going to catch me again, I say to myself. Never.

Chapter 11

I'm not strong enough to help Nate pull people up on deck and although Nate has tried to find a good reason to keep me up here, I quickly realize that I am getting in the way, hanging around the ladders. But they need help getting people organized in the hold. I have a little talk with myself.

"It is *not* Auschwitz. It's the opposite. It's a boat taking you to freedom. And if we want to get there we have to sneak away before dawn and that'll never happen unless we get organized."

So I take a deep breath and go down into the hold and try to help.

A familiar voice speaks in my ear.

"Mazel tov," it says. "You got the children here just as I said. I knew you would." I whirl around.

"Saul!" I don't know what comes over me but I throw my arms around him and hug him.

He smiles and I can see he is trying to get a good look at me in the dim light.

"I think all that sunshine and fresh air has done you a world of good," he nods.

"Like a weed, you mean," I laugh.

"No, like a beautiful little flower. A beautiful flower who's learned to laugh again! We'll talk later.

Now we have to get everyone on this boat."

"Ruth!" It is Zvi. "Some of the children won't stay in the bunks. Come and help me."

I run over to him. "I didn't know Saul would be here," I say. To me, Saul seems to *be* Palestine, in the flesh.

"Neither did I," Zvi says. "Often the organizer will stay where they're sent but Saul told me that sometimes they make the trip back and forth to Palestine, as well. It all depends where the Mossad needs them the most."

Zvi, Rivka, Fanny, Sima, Karl, and I each take a different section of the boat and usher people to their bunks as they come in. Other young people from other groups are also helping. The hold is split into two parts, a rough floor built across half of the hold, and then bunks built up from the floor in every imaginable space. Nate tells us that we'll have almost a thousand passengers on board by the time we are finished.

Finally, just as no more people can fit, Nate pokes his head down the ladder where I am working. "That's it," he says. "No one's allowed on deck until we reach the high sea. Can't have anyone suspecting us." And the ship begins to move!

For an hour or two the sailing is smooth and although it is early morning people try to sleep as no one had any rest the night before. It is quiet, almost peaceful. Then the ship begins to roll, just a little. I'm not sleeping, I'm staring up at the bunk above me, Zvi beside me, holding my hand. I am desperately trying not to think of Auschwitz, but I'm not doing too well. I'm alternately chilled or sweating and all I want to see is the sky above me and stars. I used to dream of that in Auschwitz. Dream of being able to see the stars at night when I slept. Zvi, having slept out in the open for years, is quite content to lie in a dry if crowded bunk.

The ship begins to roll heavily. My stomach starts to feel queasy. Rivka, just below me on the bunks, suddenly throws up. The smell is nauseating and before I can stop myself, I lean over the bunk and throw up, too. This must make others feel sick because soon the entire hold is full of people throwing up and the worse the smell gets the more people get sick. As I lay there, too nauseated to move, I can see people just below me trying to clean up the mess. Fanny is on her knees picking up the vomit with bare hands and putting it into cans. Then Karl is washing the area down with soap but I guess they have to ration the water because he is using very little of it. I try to get up to help, I don't want anyone to have to clean up after me like that but the ship is pitching and rolling, everyone is throwing up, the stench is unbelievable, and I end up throwing up more. I almost hit Karl.

He looks up to see who it is and when he sees it's me he shakes his head. "It'll pass, Ruth," he assures me.

The rest of the day is absolute hell. Everyone around me is sick, the children are crying, the poor few who are unaffected have the horrible job of cleaning up the mess. Zvi is amazing. He was sick shortly after me, but has dragged himself out of the bunk and is helping the others clean even as he has to stop every once in a while to be sick himself. I am moved to a lower bunk so I don't make such a mess when I throw up. If Saul should happen along now I would happily kill him. Why hadn't he just left me in Poland, anywhere so long as I wouldn't have to go through this? And the way the ship is creaking and moaning—I'm scared. What if we sink? I'll die in a miniature Auschwitz on a fool's journey to nowhere.

After what seems to be forever, a loud whistle blows.

"It's the all clear," Zvi says to me.

"The all clear!" a number of voices call. "We can go on deck."

I am too weak and nauseated to move. "Please," I plead with Zvi, "help me get up there." But then a pair of strong arms picks me up, and Saul is carrying me up the ladder and the cold air hits me, it is so fresh, so pure, so clean. Salt water sprays onto the deck and I am sure I've gone straight from hell, right up to heaven. The stars are out, the moon is rising, and Saul puts me down in a lifeboat at the back of the ship. Zvi covers me with a blanket.

"Thank you," I whisper. They both look like angels to me. Soon Rivka is beside me, and those who can make it out on deck do so. The deck is flooded with people. I gaze up at the stars above me and even though the wind blows and the boat still rolls dread-fully, I no longer feel like throwing up, just very weak.

Rivka isn't so lucky. She continues to throw up non-stop. Karl cleans up after her and the others on deck. Below deck, a cleanup squad has been organized and they've gone to work trying to gain some ground as the hold empties out. I can see Zvi throwing up over the rail and then running to help someone else who is sick. I feel useless but I'm too weak and sick to really care at this point.

The bad weather lasts and lasts. In the morning we are allowed to stay on deck but only if there are no ships in sight. If we spot another ship somehow we all have to make our way back into the holds which by now are hot and smell unbearably. There are many Orthodox on board who pray morning, afternoon, and evening, and I hope they are praying for good weather.

Actually as I hear their prayers, I remember some of them, and sometimes I find myself chanting along with them. Not that I believe God will listen, God has ignored us for years. In fact, I often wonder if God doesn't hate us. But then, almost superstitiously, I wonder if we shouldn't be nice to Him so He won't be so mean to us.

One night as our group lies in the lifeboat I say something like that and Karl just scoffs. "Don't be silly, Ruth," he says, "there is no God so you don't have to worry about pleasing or *not* pleasing Him."

I manage to lift myself up a bit, I'm starting to feel stronger. "Why is it always a Him?" I ask.

"Because He was made up by men," Karl answers, "in their image."

"That's not true," Fanny objects. "Of course God exists."

"I think," Sima says quietly, "that God exists in all of us. When we create art, or express love, or do anything beautiful, that is God."

We all look at her very surprised. Sima usually says so little, just doing her artwork and carrying out her chores. I didn't think she believed in anything.

"God is there and we must follow His commands and settle in Eretz Israel, just as the Bible tells us," Rivka says.

"You can't take the Bible literally like that," Karl scoffs. I can see this is bound to lead to a big argument between Rivka and Karl so I turn to Zvi.

"What do you think, Zvi?" I ask.

"One day," Zvi says, "a priest came to a rabbi with an invitation."

"Oh no, Zvi," I cry, "I'm serious! Not a joke!"

"Let me finish," Zvi insists and carries on.

"The priest wanted to take the rabbi to a boxing match. The rabbi agreed but had never attended one so the priest had to explain everything to him. He explained the ring, the crowd, the rules. Finally the two boxers entered the ring and just before the match started, one of the boxers crossed himself.

"'Why is he doing that?' asked the rabbi. 'What does it mean?'

"'It doesn't mean anything,' said the priest, 'if that boxer doesn't know how to fight.'"

I laugh, as does the rest of the group.

"That's what I believe," Zvi says, still smiling, "God exists. God is there. But God doesn't decide what happens here on earth; we do. God gave us free will and we have to use it. As for me, I'm going to make sure I *always* know how to fight. We will make a place where we'll all be safe," he says fiercely.

Why am I the only one who doesn't have an answer? Every single one of their answers sounds possible to me. And perhaps Zvi is right about God. But that doesn't mean I can't be mad at Him. In fact, since that day a few weeks ago when I began to wake up from my sleep I've found myself getting madder and madder. Sometimes I think I will explode in rage. I look at Sima enviously. She seems so at peace with everything. It makes me feel like throttling her!

I wake up on the third day out, to find the weather has cleared. It seems we are alone on the seas, and so, finally, we are all allowed to be out on deck during the day.

Chapter 12

It's a beautiful day. I lean over the rail and gulp deep breaths of sea air. The smell of fresh bread is everywhere. Refugee volunteers, bakers before the war, are manning two big ovens and we've had fresh bread every morning. Karl has been getting our allotment and making sure the children are fed and cared for. Yesterday I'd nibbled some food for the first time—otherwise my diet has consisted of sucking on a lemon slice. Today I'm ravenous.

I eat all of my bread, drink the small amount of water I'm allowed, and have a small bowl of stew. That's our meal, morning, noon, and night. Zvi gobbles his and we watch as the children run all over the ship, exploring, playing, having fun for the first time on the trip. Many of them have been sick, the others, bored to tears, had become cranky and impossible. Even Zvi's jokes and games had not kept them happy. They'd fought with one another and Jonathan had bitten one of the other boys in the group during a scuffle. Even the grownups had gotten into fights on the second day of bad weather— some heated enough that blows were exchanged. But today the bad tempers are disappearing with the wind.

Everyone is on deck and it is the first time I get a good sense of who I'm traveling with. I can hear many different languages—the most common being Polish; there are all ages—from newborn babies to a few very old people; and there are people from every different type of Zionist movement. I can tell because everyone is arguing and discussing why *their* movement is better than anyone else's.

A middle-aged man is playing the concertina and a group around him is singing Hebrew songs. On the other side of the deck the Orthodox are finishing their morning prayers and their chants intermingle with the other lovely melodies.

Zvi collects our paper plates and takes the empty bucket which had been full of food back to the galley. I decide to wander around the deck, so I can listen to people talk, and just to relax, as I know that soon we'll probably have to do something with the children. But for now, they're happy.

"You don't understand," I hear a voice say, "Palestine should be divided equally between Arab and Jew."

"If you think that'll work you're a dreamer," another voice answers. "Not that I disagree, I just don't see it happening that way."

I stop dead. I look. That voice. But no, I'm being silly. For the rest of my life I'm bound to see a face that looks familiar, hear a voice that sounds familiar, and I'll think it's someone from home, a friend, or family. . . .

"We can't only be practical. If we don't aim for something, it'll certainly never happen. That's what happens with *your* attitude."

"I'm just being realistic."

That voice again. I begin to push my way through the people toward the voice. My heart is hammering in my chest. I'm suddenly drenched in sweat. Of course it can't be him. He's dead. They're all dead.

I push a particularly big fellow aside. "Hey!" he exclaims. "Watch it!"

And then I see him. And at the same moment he sees me. At first he has no reaction and turns back to his conversation. Then slowly he pivots toward me, a kind of question in his eyes. After all, I was ten years old when we last saw each other. He was eleven. But I know it's him. And then his whole face changes, suddenly it's glowing, and he's moving toward me and I'm moving toward him. We stop when we reach each other.

The conversation all around us stops, like the quiet in the center of a storm. Everyone knows that a miracle is taking place. I reach up and gingerly touch his face with my fingers. He is tall, somehow he's grown, he's very skinny, his hair is pitch black and curly like mine, his eyes blue, his face gaunt. When my fingers touch his face he puts a hand over them and clasps them tight.

"Ruth," he whispers.

"Simon," I say, barely able to get the word out.

He nods.

I throw my arms around him and clutch him tight and I can feel his tears wet on my arm and everyone around us begins to clap and shout.

"Who is it, Simon, who is it?" his friends ask.

He holds my arm up like a boxer who has just won a match.

"It's my sister!"

"It's his sister!" the cry goes up all over the ship and soon Zvi is beside me and I show him Simon, I say, "It's my brother!" And those are the sweetest words that have ever come out of my mouth. "It's my brother! He's alive."

"She's alive!"

Soon the entire ship knows of our reunion and people are clapping and shouting all over the deck, and Simon and I keep hugging each other and showing each other off to each new friend who arrives. I have to introduce him to Saul and to Rivka and Fanny, who lifts him up in a huge bear hug, and Sima, who shyly shakes his hand, and Karl, and someone brings out some chocolate they've been saving in the galley and the entire deck turns into one big party. The concertina player starts a hora and everyone whirls around and Simon and I dance in the center, spinning round and round until we are dizzy and we are both laughing and crying at the same time. Then Simon takes my hand and we go over to a little corner, everyone clapping as we leave. The celebration continues without us. We sit on two little crates and for a moment neither of us speaks.

"I looked for you, Ruth," Simon says. "Everywhere."

"I looked for you, too," I say.

"Did you go back to Uncle Moishe's house?"

I nod. "The maid was wearing Mother's dress."

"Bastards," he mutters.

"I asked her if she'd seen anyone," I say.

"So did I."

"When were you there?" I ask.

"Last year," he replies. "Right after the war. Since then I've been in a D.P. camp in Germany."

"I went to Uncle's house in July." My voice is bitter. "She could have told me you'd been there. She could have."

"Never mind," he says. "Now we've found each other."

"Father?" I ask.

Simon shakes his head. "When they emptied Auschwitz, Father went on the forced march. Probably to Buchenwald."

I gasp. "But that's where I was."

"Up until then Father and I had been together but I was too sick to march," he continues, "so I stayed behind in one of the barracks. The Nazis left me for dead. Two days later the Russians came in. I joined up and fought with them 'til the end of the war." He pauses. "Mother? Hannah?"

"Gone that first day, I think," I reply. "They were

both so thin and weak from life in the ghetto. I never saw them after that first day in Auschwitz. They were in line for the gas."

He shakes his head. "And you. I thought all the Jews were marched out of Buchenwald just before it was liberated. And shot."

"I was too sick to go," I say.

"Copying your older brother again." He grins.

I grin back. "I suppose you're going to start bossing me around as if you know what's best for me."

"Of course," he says, "and you'd better listen."

"I'll listen to you the way I always did," I reply.

He laughs. "Well, that's not at all, isn't it?"

"Not at all," I agree.

I touch his shoulder. "I just can't believe you're real," I say. "I'd resigned myself that I was all alone. Totally alone. The last of our family."

"Then you haven't heard?"

"What?"

"Our Aunt Sophie, Dad's sister, she's alive in Palestine."

"No!"

Aunt Sophie had always been the meekest of the family. She'd lived under the shadow of her husband, Uncle Zev, who was a doctor in Warsaw.

"She got out through the illegal immigration," Simon continues, "through Uncle Zev's connections. The oldest daughter Mika got out with her, and now Aunt Sophie is this big Haganah organizer in

Palestine. She was the one who pulled some strings and got me out of the D.P. camp in Germany, otherwise I'd still be there."

Suddenly I have not one, but three relatives alive. It is too much. I feel quite dizzy.

"*And*," Simon adds, "you'll never guess who I bumped into in a transit camp on the way to Germany."

"Who?"

"Crazy Lille."

"Crazy Lille?"

She had been really crazy. About ten years older than us, she'd spent most of her time running around naked in the fields, an event which the boys always tried to catch, or talking loudly to herself in shul or at market.

"She's not crazy anymore."

"But how could *she* survive when sane people everywhere died?"

"She survived and is perfectly sane and got married right after the war and was already pregnant when I saw her. Not crazy anymore," he repeats.

"Maybe the world around her was too crazy even for her," I say.

"I guess so," he replies.

For a minute we are both quiet and then I start to giggle. "Crazy Lille," I repeat. And the giggle turns into a laugh. And the laugh is a real one, because it really is funny and Simon laughs too and it's the first time I can remember really laughing because I'm *happy*, not at one of Zvi's jokes, but out of sheer happiness and I didn't think I would ever feel happy again.

Suddenly I stop as I remember something.

"What?" he asks.

"I should have known," I say. "You weren't in my dream."

"What?"

"I dreamed that Mother and Father and Hannah and Joshua came to me and hugged me and told me they loved me—but you weren't there!"

Simon looks at me.

"Maybe there is something beyond this life after all," I say.

"Maybe there is," Simon agrees, his eyes once more filling up with tears.

"What is it?" I ask.

"Joshua," he says. Our older brother who always protected us.

"What?"

"They put the two of us to work in a rock quarry and if you dropped the sack they beat you or shot you. One day I was so tired I fell down and the guard saw me. Joshua picked me up and when the guard called for me, Joshua ran to him. I was too exhausted. I couldn't move. So the guard shot Joshua." He paused. His voice drops so I can barely hear him. "It was my fault, Ruth. I should be dead. Joshua should be here."

I take his hands in mine. "It's not your fault. It's the Nazis' fault."

He looks at me with a fierceness I'd never believed possible. "No one will ever treat me or my family or the Jews like that again," he vows. "I'll fight every last one of them, British, Arab, whoever gets in my way."

I start to cry again. We are alive, but what is left of us?

Chapter 13

Simon and I spend the rest of the day together, inseparable. I am so happy one minute I feel like bursting, so sad the next, remembering all we've lost, that I cry inconsolably. But I do cry. I cry out of happiness, I cry out of sadness. And I laugh, too. And we sing together and as night closes in we dance on the deck of the ship, dance and sing until everyone is hoarse. All the children dance with us, celebrating as if they'd found a brother, too. And it gives some of them hope. Even Jonathan comes up to me and says, "Maybe, somewhere in Eretz Israel there's a cousin or even a neighbor from my street—who knows?" And then others start to come up to Simon and me and tell us their stories. Little miracles, all of them. One fellow introduces himself as Mordechai.

"I went back to my town in Poland," he says, "but everything was gone. I mean everything. The entire Jewish section had been ripped down and they were paving the streets with the bricks from our homes. Out of thousands of Jews, there were none left. None! It was so cold that winter in '45 and I was walking down the street, just a little thin overcoat on, bundled up against the snow, and I passed a woman, also bundled up covered in a thick shawl. She was crying 'If only I could find my Mordechai. If only I could find my Mordechai.' I turned and ran after her and stopped her. Sure enough—it was my older sister. Can you believe it? She's married now and in a D.P. camp in Germany. She wants to go to the United States. But I had to go to Palestine. I hated to leave her. But I have to do this."

A woman comes up to us and proudly displays her husband as if he is a prize cow. "Every day," she says, "I'd go to the Jewish Agency office in the camp I was in and I'd check the lists. Every day I read about another relative confirmed dead. Every day my will to live dwindled and I began to give up hope. And then one day—there it was—Chaim's name. Right there. Alive and in a camp in Austria. I thought he'd have a heart attack when he saw me." Chaim, who was very tall and gangly, beamed at his little wife who'd probably once been fat and cheerful. Actually, despite it all, she still seemed cheerful.

And so night wears on, but we don't go down to the holds to sleep until the moon starts to set and dawn is threatening to break. When we do go to sleep, Simon and I have to separate even though I don't want to leave him for even a minute. We are in different sections though, and I still have my children to look after.

Once the children are settled in their bunks (some of them had fallen asleep on the deck and had to be carried down) they begin to clamor for me to tell them the story of me and Simon. So I tell them how I'd come all the way from Poland, and had gotten on the boat and was walking across the deck and heard a familiar voice.

"Did you know right away who it was?" Sarah asks.

"No, not right away. Not for sure. I thought it was just a voice *like* Simon's."

"Go on, go on," the others urge. They want to get to the part where I first see him.

They keep me up, making me tell the story over and over again, as if it hadn't just happened hours ago.

We go on deck in the morning to find it sunny and hot, and it feels almost like a kind of wonderful vacation. We splash seawater over one another to cool off as the day progresses—it's a heat like nothing I've ever felt before. This goes on for three days—we're allowed on deck to eat, talk, and dance, Simon and I spend as much time as possible together—and I notice that he is also paying a lot of attention to Rivka. Often Simon, Rivka, Zvi, and I sit under the stars talking well into the night.

But one afternoon a plane buzzes overhead. The whistle blows. We gather the children and everyone hurries into the holds. Have the British spotted us?

The all clear whistle blows finally, but Saul calls everyone to a meeting on the foredeck. He tells us that should we be captured and interrogated by the British there is only one answer we have to remember.

"Where were you born? Eretz Israel. Where are you coming from? Eretz Israel. As far as we're concerned you are already citizens of Eretz Israel."

A cheer rises up from the crowd.

"I must tell you," he continues, "that Haganah orders have changed. Passive resistance is no longer the order of the day. We are asked to resist the British in any way possible. You will each be separated into fighting units with a Haganah commander in charge. When, if, the British try to board us we will resist with any means at our disposal.

"Are you in agreement?" he asks the crowd. "Will you fight?"

Again everyone cheers and shouts "Yes," in all their different languages. As Saul speaks, of course, you can hear people translating for others all over the ship so there is a constant babble of voices.

"We may be taken to Cyprus," Saul warns. "And there you'll see barbed wire again."

There is an angry, unhappy muttering through the crowd.

"Now, you must all line up and go one by one into the captain's cabin where you'll get your illegal immigration certificates. Or should I say your 'perfectly legal document' so you may enter Palestine!"

At that the crowd laughs and cheers again. We organize the children and patiently stand in line. I'd never seen the captain but Nate had told us that he is an American, as are many of the crew. He isn't in his cabin when we finally get there, in fact it is Miriam who sits at a desk organizing everyone.

We are given a blue certificate called "Permit to

Enter Palestine." It is in Hebrew on one side, English on the other. I can't make out the English at all so I fill out the Hebrew side, then help the little ones fill theirs out, too. I read the certificate quickly and see that it says I've been "found qualified by the representatives of the Jewish Community of Palestine for repatriation to Eretz Israel." Miriam is signing each certificate, "Moishe ben Maimon." "Who is that?" I ask her.

"That is Maimonides's Hebrew name. He was a very famous Hebrew philosopher from the Middle Ages." She grins.

"Won't the British notice?" I ask.

She laughs. "You should see the names we signed on your illegal 'Greek' papers." She shakes her head. "They have no idea!"

We take the children out and Nate waves us over. Our group of twenty children and about five teenagers is to join up with another seventy-five young people. Nate stands on a crate and addresses us all, as he is our commander.

"Our unit will be on deck when they try to board the ship," Nate says. "Jonathan, you are old enough to be in charge of the little ones, so you will stay below with them."

Jonathan doesn't seem to know whether to be happy for the responsibility, or angry that he isn't considered old enough to go on deck.

"The rest of us must find things to throw at the

British when they try to board us. Any tools we may have, knives, forks, spoons, small pieces of wood—anything. That's all we'll have to fight with. They'll have water cannons, real cannons, guns, and, worst of all, tear gas. It's usually the gas which overcomes everyone, so be prepared. We're leaving three units in the hold so that if those of us on deck get gassed, those in the hold can come up on deck and replace us. Our main job is to keep them from getting onto the ship, and getting to the bridge. Once there, they'll take command of the ship. Any questions?"

There are none.

I'm excited that we aren't just going to let the British capture us and force us to go to Cyprus. The thought that the Haganah leaders see us all as fighters makes me feel like one—proud, almost strong.

It is Friday, Shabbat, so as the sun sets we gather on deck and listen while the Orthodox conduct the service. It is very beautiful, the sky a wash of pinks and oranges and deep blues. I notice Simon praying with some of the Orthodox militant wing, Betar. He told me he'd changed parties but it's hard to believe he's changed to such a right-wing group. After the service an older man brings out his violin and begins to sing. Everyone joins in.

> *Where are we going? Home, home.*
> *Home to a new life, to Peace and*
> *Freedom.*

Where are we going? Home. Home.
Home to the fields and meadows,
The cities and factories of a Jewish
Land.
And where is home? Stranger, can you
ask?
Home is where wandering ends, where
we live by right.
Home is Artzenu, Artzenu, our land,
our land.
Eretz Tsion Yisrael—the Land of Zion,
Israel.

No one wants to go below to the heat and smell, so once again we stay on deck for most of the night. We sleep a few hours and in the morning come up in time for the Shabbat service. The reading from the Prophets is 66 Isaiah 13, "As one whom his mother comforteth, so will I comfort you; and you shall be comforted in Jerusalem."

It seems everyone is crying by the time the portion is read—including me. Of course, since I started crying a few days ago I haven't been able to stop, and I cry over nothing and everything all the time.

Simon and I get into our first fight shortly after the service is over.

"Why Betar?" I ask him. "What's the matter with Noar Zioni?"

"I'll tell you," Simon says. "They're too soft. The

world understands one thing and one thing only, force. Who's strong? Who's weak? If the world sees we are weak, we'll *never* get our land. If they see we're strong, they'll have to give it to us."

"But Simon," I say, "I agree that we can't be weak. We can fight when attacked, of course, but should we *become* the attackers?"

Betar is aligned with the Irgun in Palestine, a militant group which launches attacks on the British to try to help them decide to leave Palestine.

"That's the only thing the British will understand," Simon says. "If it isn't dangerous for them why would they have any incentive to leave? They'd be nice and cozy and stay there forever. No, we have to make them so fearful they can't wait to get out of there."

"You'll only sway world opinion *away* from us," Zvi objects, coming to join the conversation.

"That's true," I agree. "Now we have the sympathy of the world. If the Irgun turns everyone against us, what then?"

We don't have a chance to finish our talk. The whistle blows and we have to hurry below deck. We can hear planes overhead, buzzing the ship. Every once in a while Nate comes down to report to us—no ships on the horizon, all clear for now, but the planes keep coming so we are forced to stay in the hold all day.

The heat has become almost unbearable. I have to tell the children story after story to keep them from becoming completely unruly. I make up some ghost stories set on a creaky old ship and intersperse those with their favorite, Simon and I meeting.

Finally night falls and the whistle blows. We scramble up on deck and gasp in the cool night air.

But far off in the distance, I think I see lights. When morning comes the lights turn out to be just what we have all dreaded—British warships.

Chapter 14

We are all immediately sent below deck to see if we can fool the British into believing we are a simple freighter. But, according to Nate who keeps us informed, one of the warships gets close enough to communicate by loudspeaker. They call that they know we are transporting illegals to Palestine. They can't touch us as long as we're in international waters but they shadow us all day. Finally, as the heat becomes unbearable in the holds, the captain decides there is no use trying to keep up the façade. The all clear whistle blows and we are allowed on deck. At the same time the captain raises a flag with the Star of David. Spontaneously the entire crowd breaks out singing Hatikva, the song we consider our national anthem even if we don't have a nation yet.

Rather than being depressed, most of the passengers become more and more elated because we are getting closer and closer to Palestine. They dance and sing. I join in, too. Even I am beginning to want to get there. Those British warships remind me how important it is to have a place I can call home. And it finally occurs to me that I'll never have to wander from place to place, lost, again. And now that I have Simon, we can start a new life, with family.

As darkness falls our captain tries to elude the warships. He maneuvers left and right, twists and turns, sometimes going in circles but they catch us in huge spotlights and we are never fully able to escape from those circles of light that stick to us like glue.

In the morning, over our loudspeakers, we are told that we are approaching the three-mile limit. The British destroyers begin to close in. Our group follows Nate onto the deck. I notice that Saul and many of the crew have changed into shabby old clothes so the British won't be able to tell them from the rest of us. Certainly the worst thing would be for the Haganah leaders to be arrested and interrogated. I am terribly nervous, but elated, too. Finally I am going to be given a chance to fight back.

In my hands are little pieces of board which I chipped off a crate, and some cutlery. Everyone holds whatever they've been able to find. As I look out across the water at the warships I see land in the distance. It's the shores of Eretz Israel! A cheer goes up from everyone on board, broken by a British voice coming to us over a loudspeaker.

"You have entered the territorial waters of Palestine. We are going to send a boarding party. We advise you to be reasonable and act wisely. You know our strength is greater than yours. We shall treat you well on condition you do not oppose us."

At that point, as we draw closer and closer to what Saul tells us is the northern coast of Palestine, the captain decides to make a run for it. He puts on a full burst of power and heads for shore. The excitement on board is incredible. One of the warships draws along, boarding rafts on its sides. These rafts can be dropped onto our ship and make an easy bridge for their soldiers, who are dressed in gas masks, rubber suits, steel helmets, and already have big truncheons out. I take a deep breath. They certainly look scary. And I'm not looking forward to the gas. It brings back too many memories of other gas that has been used on the Jews. But I have no time to think any further. They drop the rafts, and the soldiers begin to move onto our ship.

We throw everything at them we can. I let go with my boards and cutlery, Zvi throws nuts and bolts, Nate chucks a huge pail. It is such a fierce onslaught that the British actually back off, some of their soldiers hurt, and retreat to their ship. Their destroyer veers away. I can't believe it. We've won. For the moment. But then another destroyer pulls up beside us. This one sprays us with clouds of gas from its hoses. I can't catch my breath. My eyes burn and my throat burns and my knees buckle underneath me. I fall to the ground in a kind of swoon, not quite unconscious but unable to move.

"The captain's lowering the booms!" a voice exclaims near me. No soldiers will be able to board near us, anyway. It's a horrible feeling lying here unable to do anything to help.

"They're boarding on the foredeck," someone yells. "Get a unit over there!"

My head is beginning to clear. Zvi is near me and he helps me to my feet. I'm still too groggy to move but Zvi goes to the foredeck to help, as does anyone who can. He's back in a few minutes.

"Eight soldiers got on board," he says, talking very fast, "but our unit from below easily overpowered them. Simon and some of the others wanted to shoot them but Saul let them jump overboard."

"Simon wanted to shoot them?" I repeat in disbelief. And then I remember that he watched a Nazi shoot Joshua in cold blood and I realize that he's lost all his compassion. I can't blame him but I wish it weren't so.

"We're winning, Ruth," Zvi says, "and look how close we are to shore!" We are the lengths of a few city blocks away, I'd say. I can see a beach, with lots of people on it, lots of activity.

The first destroyer moves near us again and sprays more gas, this time on the foredeck, not near those of us on the stern. And then they open fire, spraying the deck with bullets. Most are aimed over our heads but some of our people are hit. I hear cries and screams, both from the gunfire and the gas. I have my strength back now and am ready to fight again. I see some bodies fall but can't tell who they are. But then, under cover of fire, the British soldiers manage to secure some rafts and make their way on board ship. So we fight them, hand to hand. They hit us with their truncheons and we hit back with fists and anything we can throw. Fanny begins to pull up floorboards and we throw them at the soldiers.

I hear someone cry out and I look around. It is Zvi and he calls me over. On the deck, a bullet through his chest, is Saul. He is covered in blood.

"No!" I scream. I fling myself down beside him, putting my hands on his chest, trying to stop the bleeding.

Zvi grabs my hands away.

"It's no use," he says. "He's dead."

"No!" I cry again.

"He died for a reason," Zvi says to me. "To get us here. Come on, Ruth, we have to help. There's nothing we can do for him now."

All my rage suddenly explodes into a red mass like blood and I want to hurt them, all of them who have hurt us, and I grab a piece of board from Fanny and throw myself into the fight, flailing at the soldiers with my plank, hitting as many as I can. I have strength I never knew was possible.

The British are trying to get to the bridge and slowly they make their way there, but, without warning, with an incredible thud and lurch the ship beaches!

"We're on shore! We're on shore!" The cry goes up.

"Into the water," Nate screams. "Everyone swim for shore!"

Simon finds me and grabs my hand. He pulls me to the railing, almost drags me up, and we jump. Of course, I can't swim, they don't give lessons in concentration camps, but the most amazing thing happens. There are already people in the water. Not people from the boat. People from land. And they pass us from hand to hand, the British on their warships helpless to stop us. And as I stagger onto the beach I see hundreds of young people. They are waiting, holding dry clothes. I am taken by a young woman, stripped right there of my wet clothes and put into shorts and a shirt, just like those she is wearing. My damp papers are taken out of my pocket and thrown into a pile with others until a huge blue mound rises up out of the sand. Everywhere around us more and more trucks arrive, and their passengers, Jewish Palestinians, mingle with us.

The pile of papers is set on fire. Relieved, I see Zvi close by, and Simon, and most of my group. Not the children though. They wouldn't be allowed to jump from the ship. Soon there are thousands of locals on the beach with us and we are interspersed with them and they all begin to sing and dance the hora!

By then British soldiers are arriving by truck. They surround us all and pour onto the beach. One pulls me out of the group and demands to know if I have come off the ship. They begin to do that with everyone. I answer in perfect Hebrew that I live in Eretz Israel, and they are so frustrated because they can't tell the illegals from the legals.

How has the Haganah gotten people here so fast? I'm just amazed. It is incredible. I ask a young Palestinian next to me.

She grins. "We heard from your ship you were on your way," she says, her voice low. "All the kibbutzim in the area went on alert and were told to get here as fast as possible—bodies to confuse the British. We even wet our hair so they can't tell who's just come off the boat." She squeezes my hand. "You're home now!"

I can barely believe it. They are willing to risk everything for us. I actually feel wanted, like I'm worth something, like I'm meant to be here. They've protected us with their own lives.

Finally, in frustration, the British decide to arrest as many as were on the boat, one thousand people they announce, Palestinians and refugees alike. I'm one of them, as are Zvi and Nate and Miriam and the rest of our group. But not Simon. Somehow Simon manages to get away.

We are put on trucks and driven to Haifa. It's on the truck that the elation slowly leaves me, the anger leaves me, and I start to think about Saul. But I can't cry. I can't cry.

Deep inside me something says don't feel anything, go back to sleep, when you feel, it hurts. When you love, people die. You're in Eretz Israel. This is where you should be. But don't dare to be happy. Don't dare.

Chapter 15

I think it is right that it was Saul who sent me on a journey which woke me up, and now it is Saul who is allowing me to go back to sleep. Zvi stays beside me all night as we are driven to the port of Haifa. We are forced to wait on the trucks until the morning, and then they spray us with some horrible delousing pesticide. We're pushed up a gangplank onto a different boat. I am questioned, briefly, by a polite young British officer but I answer that I am from Eretz Israel so they can do nothing. They decide to send us all on to Cyprus.

The children are already on the boat under Jonathan's supervision. They run to us and hug us. Many of the passengers who'd been too old or sick to jump are there too, as are those who've been captured. No one is depressed. Everyone feels a great victory has been won over the British. And many of our new companions assure us that it won't be long before the British have to return all of us to Palestine—because obviously many of them belong there and it is certainly against their rights to lock them up in Cyprus.

We arrive in Cyprus that afternoon, the sun beating down on us like a weapon. We disembark on a sandy beach, old stone walls rising above us.

Everyone resists being taken off the ship so it takes them a long time to drag us one by one onto shore, then put us on trucks. The trucks are covered so I can't see much until we are ordered out. We clamber into a mass of sand and dirt, a tent city erected behind barbed wire.

I start to get angry, then remind myself that I have to sleep. Anger is a feeling, too.

A week goes by and I hardly notice. I take care of the children, do my job, don't bother anyone. I don't talk, I think that's best. Zvi stays with me all the time and sometimes, often, I feel something stirring in me when he looks at me or holds my hand but I stomp on it, I crush it. I won't let it emerge. After all, Zvi could easily be killed tomorrow. Or Simon. Sometimes I consider killing myself. It wouldn't be that different than now. I could just go to sleep *all* the time and I wouldn't have to fight that little part of myself that wants to wake up, come alive. It takes a lot of effort to fight that. I'm not sure I want to make that effort any more.

Rivka comes into the tent and sits down beside me. She's been working with Sima doing artwork with the children. I'm lying on my bunk staring at nothing.

"I've heard from Simon," she says.

That surprises me.

"You have?"

She nods. "He's arranged for us to escape."

"He *has*?" I don't understand how Simon could

have arranged that in such a short time. And then I think of Aunt Sophie. I look at Rivka. "Us," she said. And I think about the time they'd spent together on the boat.

"We love each other," she says.

I snort.

"What is it?" she asks.

"Nothing," I reply. "I'll stay here. You go."

"You don't think we can love each other?" she challenges me.

"Sure, of course you can. But he could be dead tomorrow," I warn. "Or you could."

"And is that a reason *not* to love someone?" she asks.

"Yes," I reply. "Yes, it is."

"What a coward you are, Ruth," she says. "I never realized."

A coward? Me? After what I'd been through?

"I'm no coward," I reply. "I'm just not stupid, like you."

"You're a coward," she says, "afraid to feel anything in case you get hurt. Well, look around. Haven't we all been hurt? Don't you think it takes courage to be happy, to feel, to love? Don't you think it costs us all?"

I stare at her. "Fine, I'm a coward. I'd rather be a coward than to have to feel anything ever again. Go away," I say.

"Zvi is going, too," she adds. "The three of us. Tonight. At 1:00 A.M. Be ready."

"I'm not going," I insist.

She gets up and leaves the tent, only to be followed in by Nate.

He sits beside me on the cot.

"I've been sent to take down your story," he says. "We have everyone in the group but you."

"No," I answer.

"Even the smallest have done it," Nate scolds. "Don't be difficult."

And then I realize that I'm getting angry, and to be difficult means I must feel something so I agree.

I can tell him. Why not? I am asleep. Nothing touches me. I feel nothing. I begin. I talk for a long time, tell him of our family in Kurov, the move to the ghetto, the camps, then I get to the point where Saul finds me and suddenly my voice leaves me. Finally I say, "'*Amcha*.' That was the first word he said to me."

"You *are* of the people," Nate says to me. "And we need you. I've helped organize your escape," he adds.

"Why?" I ask, genuinely puzzled.

"I saw you fight." He smiles. "We need to train as many fighters as we can for when the British leave Palestine. We may have a war with the Arabs then."

"I was just mad," I say, shaking my head.

"We all loved Saul," Nate replies. "Do you know how important each and every one of us was to him?"

I nod. I don't want to talk about him. A thick feeling is starting in my throat.

"When he saw how you'd changed, when he saw

ou on the boat he came to me and he said, 'Nate, what happened to Ruth? She's like a little sick animal that's finally become whole and healthy.' He was so happy."

"Was he?" I ask.

"Yes, he was. He thought you were wonderful. And he would just hate to see you now. He wouldn't want his Ruth. He was willing to die so you and me and Miriam and all the others could come to Eretz Israel to live. Not to mourn. Not to die inside. To live. To be happy."

"It's too dangerous," I whisper to Nate. "Too dangerous."

"Ruth. If I die tomorrow, I'll be dead. But while I'm here, I want to be alive. One or the other. Not the state you're in."

"I can't, Nate, I can't." I am pleading with him. "Don't make me."

"You can, Ruth. And no one can make you." He puts down his pen. "Don't you think Saul would have wanted you to cry for him? Almost all of Haifa went to his funeral. You were his friend. Can't you spare a tear?"

He gets up then and leaves.

I spend the rest of the day lying in the tent. People come in and out, sometimes the children jump on my cot and beg for a story but I am wandering inside, wandering through my past, trying to see if there is a place there strong enough to hold me.

Zvi comes in and brings me some dinner. "Hav
you heard, Ruth?" he says.

I nod.

"Must be your aunt," Zvi says. "Nice of Simon
include me."

"I know why they're doing this," I say. "They'r
worried about me. They think I'm going to kill myse
or something. They want to keep me too busy t
think."

"We're all worried about you," Zvi says. "And s
what if that's why they're doing it? They love you. I
that such a crime? They care about you. Come o
Ruth. I'll be scared to go without you. In fact, I won
go without you."

"Don't be silly," I say. "You have to go. This is you
dream. Tonight you'll be in Palestine."

"Not without you," Zvi says, his blue eyes starin
into mine. "I mean it. If you stay, so do I."

He's so stubborn. He's so irritating. Well, I won
be responsible for ruining the only thing he's eve
wanted.

"Fine," I sigh. "I'll go."

I eat, I sit with the children, and finally, becaus
they beg me, I tell them one last time the story c
Simon and me and our meeting on the boat.

Then Zvi begins to talk. I expect another of his joke:
Instead he tells the children a version of an old story b
Gorky and as he speaks I remember my mother readin
me the story, how it had scared me and thrilled me at th

ame time, in fact how I'd started to make up my own
tories shortly after. Had I told Zvi about that? I don't
think so.

"A small tribe," Zvi says, "fled into a swampy forest
to get away from their enemies. They couldn't find
their way out, and finally, after many years, stopped
trying. They gave up hope and slowly began to die. A
young boy, his heart full of courage, decided that he
must act. He convinced the tribe to follow him in a last
effort to leave the darkness behind and to find the sun
and freedom. They had a terrible journey. They
encountered wolves, wild animals, monsters even.
There was nothing to eat, they grew hungry and weak.
They blamed the boy for taking them on an impossible
mission and began to threaten to kill him. He turned
to them, tore his chest, pulled out his heart, and held
it above his head. The heart glowed, full of light, and
as he held it, he marched, the tribe following him.
Finally, they emerged from the forest into the sunlight.
The boy crumpled to the ground and because he was
suffering terribly, a young man eased the boy's way to
the next world by stepping on his heart. The heart
shattered into tiny bits and flew into the sky to become
millions of sparks which shine and show those who
seek the light, the way."

What is the matter with my face? It's wet. And I
realize I'm crying. Tears are pouring from me as I
think of Saul and my family and all those who died as
little sparks of light, showing me the way.

Chapter 16

Nate leads us through the camp to an area behind the kitchens. This is where trucks go in and out bringing food and supplies. It's also where the barbed wire is neatly cut so we can slip through onto the other side. The guards' rounds have been carefully monitored and we make it out with no problem—until a dog begins to bark. The camp is full of dogs which the refugees have adopted as pets and obviously one of them has heard us. This starts the others barking.

"Damn," Nate swears. "The British will be here in no time to investigate this racket. Look, you three will have to go on alone. I'll stay here and pretend I'm working late in the kitchens."

"Go where?" I say.

"Follow the road until you reach the orange grove," Nate instructs us, "then move into the center of the grove and wait. If all is clear get as close to the house as possible. When the lights blink on and off once that's your signal to head down to the water. A boat will be waiting."

We can hear a Jeep coming.

"Go!" he hisses.

We race across the road and down into a ditch on the other side. We lie flat, barely breathing until the ruck passes us. We can hear running now too, and oices, Nate's in particular raised in indignation. We lon't dare move while the voices are so close. As the ninutes drag on, the voices seem to come from further nd further away.

"Now?" Zvi asks.

"Now," I agree.

He lifts his head and looks around.

The sky is cloudless, a half moon in the sky, enough ight to see our way. The flashlight I hold also helps. Ve move as quickly as we can, single file, me in the ead along the road.

"Get down," Rivka warns, "I hear something." Again we flatten ourselves but this time the incline eside the road is shallow and all we can do is pray hey don't see us. Zvi grabs my hand as we lay in the lirt. His hand is strong and warm, reassuring. The eep races past, probably going too fast to notice us. Maybe Nate has made up some story which has put hem off our trail.

We scramble along the road searching for any kind of cover. Finally we see a stand of trees and we make ur way behind those. Just as well, as another Jeep comes along, this one driving slowly, a large beamed lashlight grazing the air. We each flatten ourselves ehind a tree. The Jeep slows even further, then just as I'm about to believe we've been discovered, it moves on.

"This is getting very irritating," I whisper to Zvi.

"Most annoying," he says, mimicking the sound of British officers.

I burst out laughing, which I didn't mean to do at all, and Rivka smacks me on the shoulder.

"Don't get silly," she warns. "I intend to get to Simon, *tonight*."

"Wonderful sister-in-law you'll make," I snap at her. "Beating up on a poor defenseless thing like me!"

"Come on," Zvi says, "looks like it's clear for the moment." We continue on. I'm getting terribly thirsty. The air is still warm and a light wind blows the sand up and around us.

"Is that the grove ahead?" I say. I see a mass of dark forms which I can only assume are trees. We hurry ahead and I beam my light on the trees—it is an orange grove. I've never seen one before. And there are oranges on the trees. Amazing.

We move into the center of the grove, all the time looking for lights.

"It's huge," Rivka says, "how will we ever find our way?"

"It certainly would help to have Nate here," Zvi mutters. "We could wander around here all night."

"Don't be silly," I say. "All we have to do is think logically. We know the sea is ahead of us, there," I say, pointing, "so I suggest we walk to the sea end of the orchard, then walk away from the road until we find the house."

"Sounds like a good plan to me," Zvi says.

"Me too," Rivka agrees.

We travel through the orchard for what seems like forever but it is probably just under an hour of walking when I finally can hear and smell the water. We turn then and begin to move well away from the road and finally notice the lights of a house in the distance.

"I hope that's the right house," I whisper. "I'd hate to sit here all night waiting for a signal that might never come."

"It must be," Zvi says. "Come on. Let's get closer."

We creep toward the house until we have it in good view. A back light is on, as is the front porch light, both of which we can see as the house is on an angle to us.

"That's it," Zvi decides. "Good for you, Ruth. You got us here with no problem—no wonder Nate wants them to train you for the Haganah."

I put down my flashlight, reach overhead, and pick an orange. I place the peels in my pockets so no British soldier will see any traces of us tomorrow. Zvi and Rivka do the same. We bite into the juicy sweetness of the fruit, probably the most wonderful taste in the entire world.

Rivka sits away from us under a tree. As if she wants this moment to herself. Zvi kneels beside me and takes my hand. He holds it to his chest and I can feel his bones so close to the skin and I can feel his heart racing.

"It's going to happen, Zvi," I say to him. "You're going to be in Eretz Israel."

"Yes," he says and he pulls me closer to him. "But my heart is not beating only because of that."

I am ready to laugh, to tease him for sounding like a character from those romantic novels Hannah used to read aloud to me, but something in his tone stops me. After all, my heart is racing too and it's not *only* because of the adventure we are on. I can feel the heat of his skin through his shirt. He moves toward me and kisses me. I kiss him back.

"I love you, Ruth," he whispers. "You are a warrior."

I throw my arms around him and hold him tight.

"I could die tonight," I say. "Then where will you be?"

"I can't think about that," he says fiercely. "We only have now. Nobody really has more than that. The difference is, we *know* it."

I want to tell him how I feel but I'm so scared. Terrified. If I say it, who knows what calamity might befall me?

"You've lived through all this, Ruth. Do you know how strong that makes you? Ruth, it takes more work to be afraid than to ride the fear, to live with the fear, to accept it. Please, Ruth," he pleads in my ear. "Please."

"I love you, Zvi." I whisper and then I feel as if my whole body is full of desire and love and—and hope. The craziest word of all.

We are so busy kissing each other that Rivka smacks me again to get my attention.

"Hey, you idiots," she says, but I can hear in her voice she is happy for us, "it's the signal. The lights just went on and off."

"Fine soldiers we'll make," I admonish Zvi.

This time he leads the way, past the house down to the sea. We scramble toward the beach and sure enough there is a boat moored in the water a few hundred yards away, and a young man kneeling in the sand waiting.

We rush up to him and he greets us with "Shalom."

We return the greeting. He has life jackets for us and we put them on. He motions for us to follow him and he swims out ahead of us. The thought of swimming to the boat in the dark does not appeal to me. It scares me in fact. And then I remember Zvi's words. That's all right. I can be scared. I'll always be scared. That will never go away. But that won't stop me. So I take a deep breath and plunge in, Zvi and Rivka right behind me.

It takes us about five minutes to paddle out to the boat. There is another person on board who pulls us in. We settle ourselves on the bottom of the small power craft and the fellow who pulled us in starts the motor. The boat takes off like a shot, the speed shocking me.

Zvi is beside himself with excitement, I can tell. His enthusiasm is contagious and I find myself dying to get there, too. We cut through the night and the water until finally the boat slows and our driver says, "Have a good swim. Good luck."

"Thank you," we answer and we follow our guide back into the water. It is a short swim to shore. We reach the beach and see a small Jeep waiting for us.

"Hurry," our guide says. We take off our jackets, give them to him, he hands us over to our new driver. Rivka gets in front, Zvi and I in back. "Change into the dry clothes I've left there," the driver instructs us.

"Change into dry clothes immediately," Mother chided me, as I came in soaking wet after a swim in the pond not too far away from our house. It was chilly that day but Simon had dared me, so obviously I had to do it. And then he had to, as well. Mother made me sit down and eat hot chicken soup and she scolded me for hours about how I'd catch pneumonia for sure, about how I'd be lucky just to escape with a cold, about how I should have been home doing chores anyway! And when Simon came in she started on him. And she made us eat extra at dinner to ward off the diseases stalking us and kissed us as she berated us.

If I forget the bad, I have to forget the good, too. The memories are all I have now of my family. And I don't want to lose them.

I change quickly. The driver takes our wet clothes and puts them underneath the seat. Then we set off.

We drive for about half an hour until we turn down a road, to a gate. The driver gets out, opens the gate, waves to the guards on watch, and we move into a small complex of buildings. He stops the Jeep and we clamber out.

Zvi hugs me and whirls me around. And then we're taken into a small building where the lights are still on. Simon is sitting at a table, waiting for us. He leaps up, races to me first, and gives me a huge hug. Then he and Rivka kiss. He hugs Zvi, too. Then the four of us stand there, staring at one another.

"Welcome home," Simon says.

Author's Note

THIS IS A STORY BASED ON REAL EVENTS. NEVERTHELESS FOR THE SAKE OF DRAMA I HAVE TAKEN SOME LIBERTIES. FOR INSTANCE, NO SHIP THAT I READ ABOUT WAS *BOTH* ATTACKED *AND* MANAGED TO BEACH ON PALESTINE'S SHORE BUT EACH EVENT DID HAPPEN SEPARATELY. I SIMPLY COMBINED THEM FOR GREATER EFFECT. MY READERS OFTEN WRITE TO ASK IF A SPECIFIC CHARACTER IS "REAL." THE ANSWER IS THAT NO CHARACTER IS MODELED AFTER ONE SPECIFIC PERSON I READ ABOUT, RATHER MY CHARACTERS ARE MODELED ON MANY DIFFERENT PEOPLE I BOTH READ ABOUT AND INTERVIEWED.

FROM THE TIME THE WAR ENDED IN 1945, TO MAY OF 1948, 69,000 JEWS TRAVELED TO PALESTINE BY SEA, ILLEGALLY.